FACE FRONT

MILLIE MOORE

WestBow°
PRESS
A DIVISION OF THOMAS NELSON
& ZONDERVAN

WestBow Press books may be ordered through booksellers or by contacting:

WestBow Press
A Division of Thomas Nelson & Zondervan
1663 Liberty Drive
Bloomington, IN 47403
www.westbowpress.com
1 (866) 928-1240

ISBN: 978-1-4908-2716-2 (sc)
ISBN: 978-1-4908-2717-9 (hc)
ISBN: 978-1-4908-2715-5 (e)

Library of Congress Control Number: 2014903499

Printed in the United States of America.

WestBow Press rev. date: 2/27/2014

DEDICATIONS

With a grateful heart, this book is dedicated:

To my husband, Michael Cleveland, you are my spiritual leader and teacher, my greatest love, my sounding board, my best friend and playmate. Michael, I thank you for being the wonderful man of God you are, for the grace and mercy you show me, and for the unconditional love we share. You are answered prayer, and more than I dared hope for. I love you.

To my mother, Betty Woodard, when I was going through a difficult time in my life, you gave me a book and encouraged me to 'lose myself in the story'; from that day forward, I've been hooked on reading. I would not be here today, sharing this story, if it wasn't for you. Mommy dearest, you are a precious, funny lady. I appreciate that you are always there for me. I love you.

To my father, Gary Woodard, you have always been a source of stability in my life. You sparked my love for travel at an early age and through it expanded my experiences in life and with that, my imagination. Thank you daddy; I love you.

To my family, including my siblings, Wanda Delgado, Doreen "Reenie" Brown, Lynne and Jerry Kleven, my Nephews and Nieces, Justin, Jessica, Brooke, Danielle, Jory, Raymond "Raymie", Garrett and Quinn, my Great-Nephew and Great-Nieces, Jacob, Emma and Avery, my sons, Thomas and Christopher, my daughter-in-law, Jackie and my Grandson Hayden, when I think about all of life's events we've shared over the years, I realize what an amazing, tight-knit, fun-loving, dysfunctional family we are. I am so grateful for the experiences we've shared; I wouldn't change a thing. I thank each of you for providing me with enough material to write well into my retirement years! I love you all.

To my in-laws, Donna and Virginia "Ginny Dare" Cleveland, I thank you for embracing me, not as an in-law, nor an outlaw, but as a precious sister and daughter. Thank you for opening your hearts to me and making me a special part of your family.

To my best gal pals, whom I loving refer to as my "fabulous four", Randi "Miranda" Callahan, Judy Karp, Pauline Isabelle and Gina Leeser. I realize to have so many people in my life that I call friend, is truly a gift, but to have four women in my life, that I call best friend, is not to be taken lightly, it serves as proof that I am truly blessed. I am so grateful for each and every moment in time we've shared; the laughter and tears, the great victory and the deep loss, we've spanned decades together, and I thank you from the bottom of my heart for sticking by me, through the thick and the thin, offering your love and support. I love each of you, in a very special way.

Last, but far from least, to Samantha Pignataro; one of my main characters is named after you. She too is beautiful, smart and funny. And like you, life has dealt her some pretty sour lemons, yet she continually chooses to make sweet lemonade! Sammie, I am so proud of the woman you've become and the amazing mommy you are. I have always loved, and appreciated your generous heart, and I truly admire your spirit of accomplishment! You will always be like a daughter to me. I miss you and love you lots.

ACKNOWLEDGEMENTS

"The friend in my adversity I shall always cherish most. I can better trust those who helped to relieve the gloom of my dark hours than those who are so ready to enjoy with me the sunshine of my prosperity."

Ulysses S. Grant

With appreciation and special thanks:

To my husband, Michael Cleveland, thank you handsome, for cooking, cleaning and doing laundry, all of this in an effort to support me, so I could sit at my computer, for endless hours, and chase my dream. I love you.

To my parents, Gary and Betty Woodard, you always seem to put my needs ahead of your own; I'm grateful. I love you both.

To my sister, Wanda Delgado, you have supported my every endeavor. You have been my business partner, my sounding board, my worst critic and my biggest fan. No matter what, you have always believed in me. Thank you Sissy, I sincerely appreciate all you have done for me. I love you.

To my best friend, Randi "Miranda" Callahan, your generosity has no limit. I thank you for all you have done to lift me up and support me. Miranda, you are a precious gem, and I am grateful you're in my life. I love you.

To Doreen "Reenie" Brown, Cheri Weidman, Catreena Speech and LaMont Fells, you helped bring this book to fruition, by serving as my proof reader, my sounding board, and my encourager; I sincerely thank each of you.

To Jim Chapin, thank you for generously sharing your amazing skills in photography and website design. I sincerely appreciate you, my long time friend.

To Shirley McAlister, my editor, thank you for your input, encouragement and guidance. You were a pleasure to work with.

PROLOGUE

He sat in his private office, staring at the documents that revealed the devastating truth about the day he was born. He could feel the jealousy, of the unfair twist of fate, burning inside him. He reviewed his plan in his mind once more, checking it for flaws. There were none; it was perfect. He played with the silver coin in his hand, circled it around his fingers, making it disappear and reappear like an amateur magician. He balanced the coin on his thumb and flicked it into the air. "Heads they die." He said as he watched the coin spin. It landed on top of his desk, heads up, there was no other option. He drew a deep breath and felt the rush of his greatest gamble. He knew he was about to change the course of his life, and if he lost, he would not be able to change it back.

"Jealousy is, I think, the worst of all faults because it makes a victim of both parties."

Gene Tierney

CHAPTER 1

He leaned in closer to the windshield, trying to keep the road in focus. The wipers swung back and forth in perfect sync, like dueling pendulums, straining under the pace. He could hear the sound of hard rain beating against the dull-gray-Ford rental car. Normally, he would curse this harsh weather, but tonight, he was grateful for it. The streets would be deserted, and the darkness would provide the cover he needed; the thought made him smile.

Pulling over to the curb, at the edge of a park, he turned off his headlights. He tugged at the ball cap he wore to shield his face. After shutting off the interior light, he grabbed his umbrella and opened the door. It was a seven-minute walk to her house. He had timed it to be sure. He would be soaking wet by the time he got there. *Perfect.* He thought as he hung his head, hunched his shoulders, and began his trek.

The tap on the back door startled her just a bit. That pleased him. When she peered through the window he tilted his head back to reveal his face; pale blue eyes and dirty blond hair, soaking wet.

"Oh, dear!" she hurried to open the door. "What are you doing out in this weather?" Her high pitched voice was a shrill to his ear.

"Car trouble," he was careful not to say too much.

"You're soaked! Did you walk? I'll get you a towel." She hurried to the linen closet, not waiting for his reply.

He walked around the kitchen and into the living room surveying her house. Plush, high-dollar furnishings filled the room, signed and numbered works of art hung on every wall, Waterford, Hummel, and a dozen other collectibles filled every shelf and table top. *She's a millionaire hoarder*, he thought with a sarcastic laugh.

She had been knitting. He could tell by the way the yarn and needles lay on the arm of her chair. He reached down and tapped the needles with a gloved finger. When they fell to the floor, he coaxed them under the chair with his foot. *Out of her reach*, he reasoned to himself. The evening news reported the weather loud enough for the neighbors to hear. He resisted the urge to lower the volume.

"Here you are. Take off your coat and hat; they're soaking wet. I'll go start some hot water for tea." She instructed.

"No; that's not necessary." He was quick to reply. He didn't want to get comfortable; comfort was a luxury, he didn't have time for luxuries. "I called Madison." He continued. "She'll be here shortly to pick me up."

"Maaaadison, huh?" She stretched out her daughter-in-law's name for emphasis. "Are you two having a spat? Give in, child. Madi always wins, and you know it." There was humor in her voice.

"Yes, you are observant," he said with an easy smile. He tripped up, and he knew it the moment he said it, but she justified it for him. Mothers always make excuses for their sons.

"I thought Madi told me you were away on business until Thursday. Did your meetings get cancelled?" She asked.

"Mmm-hmm," he mumbled, remaining vague. As she returned to her favorite chair, he tried to look busy drying himself off with the towel. He walked into the kitchen and hung the towel on the back door. *Can't forget to take that with me when I go,* he thought. As he walked back into the living room, he picked up a throw pillow from the couch.

He walked up behind her chair and in one swift movement, he gripped a handful of shiny, silver curls, pulled her head back and pushed the pillow over her face. Her eyes were wild with fear and confusion as she tried to wiggle free. "It will be easier if you don't fight me," he said. Her eyes locked on his, and suddenly she understood. He pressed down hard, forcing the soft, fluffy pillow to

3

fill her mouth and nostrils. Her frail arms flailed aimlessly, but she was too old and weak to fight.

"Please God!" She pleaded, in a muffled, incoherent voice. "Help my poor son," she prayed, as she gave up her life.

CHAPTER 2

"What do we have?" Detective Delgado asked Officer Ryan. "Looks like an open-and-shut case; died of natural causes."

"Adele Pruitt Montgomery," Officer Ryan read from his fact sheet. "Eighty-three years of age. Husband, Edward Montgomery, deceased. Son, Steven Montgomery, not yet notified. Neighbor, a Ms. Pauline Dore, said she walked with Ms. Montgomery every morning, and when Ms. Montgomery didn't answer the front door, Ms. Dore came around to the back door to make sure Ms. Montgomery was all right. Ms. Dore could see Ms. Montgomery through the glass window. Ms. Dore knocked on the glass, and when Ms. Montgomery did not respond, Ms. Dore called us." He lowered his fact sheet and glanced around. "Nothing suspicious," he observed.

Detective Delgado walked around the room, taking pictures and notes. The knitting needles caught his attention. It stuck him as odd that they were under the chair. *Probably nothing*, he thought, but he took pictures of them from two different angles just to be sure.

Officer Ryan tried to stay out of Detective Delgado's way. He stood near the fireplace and watched him work the scene. A picture on the mantle caught his eye. It was a girl dressed in full riding gear, sitting on her horse. There was something about her lively hazel eyes and broad smile that captured him. *She's a beauty*, he thought.

"Hey, Ryan, coroner's here." Detective Delgado pointed out. "You comin'?"

"Yep." Officer Ryan wished he could stay and check out the rest of the mantle pictures; so many of them were of the girl on the horse. She caught his curiosity. Besides, he wasn't in any hurry to get back on the street.

"Okay, we're outta here. Good job on your workup." Delgado said, giving Officer Ryan a gentle smack on the back of his head.

"Thanks." He replied, elbowing Delgado's arm away.

CHAPTER 3

Madison tugged at the blinds just enough to peek out, hopefully without being seen. The officer standing on her porch flashed his badge in her direction. She got the message and hurried to open the door. Still holding the basket of laundry under one arm and the knob of the door with the other she tried, without success, to sound normal. "Can I help you?" It came out much too breathless. *Darn*, she thought; she wasn't off to a good start.

"Madison Montgomery?" The officer inquired.

"Yes. I'm Madison Montgomery," she confirmed.

"Is Mr. Montgomery home?"

"No. He's on a business trip," she replied in a tentative voice; just as she'd rehearsed.

"When will he return?" The officer pressed.

"Can I help you?" she repeated, this time sounding a little indignant. *Good job Madi*, she thought to herself.

"Ma'am, I'm afraid I have some bad news for you and Mr. Montgomery."

"Bad news?" she tried to sound confused and a little afraid. She didn't want him to come in, so she kept her position at the door, using the laundry basket to fill in the gap.

When she finally closed the door, a grueling twelve minutes had passed. Her hip and shoulder hurt from balancing the laundry basket for so long. "Overzealous, newbie cop!" she spat as she reached for her cell phone. She touched "favorites" on her Droid, scrolled down to her husband's name, and tapped the green phone symbol to dial him. Expecting him to be in a meeting, she was surprised when he answered.

"Good morning beautiful!" He was always so happy. How could that be? *Nobody is that happy all the time!* She was in a foul mood. That stiff, by-the-book cop set her off.

"Steven," she replied in her best sullen voice.

"Madi, what's wrong?"

"Steven, it's your mom. She's passed." Madison heard the deep breath he took as he tried to maintain his composure. When he finally spoke, his voice was barely audible.

"I'm on my way home. I love you." Steven hung up the phone before she could reply.

CHAPTER 4

Samantha sat on the bed in her dorm room swiping, with the back of her hand, at the tears that ran down her cheeks. She flipped through family pictures she kept in a keepsake box, laughing at the memories and crying over her most recent loss. "Oh, Gran." She sighed at a picture of an elderly woman blowing out the candles on her eightieth birthday cake.

Samantha knew this day would come; Gran was getting up there in years, but still the news dealt a hard blow to her heart. She picked up another picture; this one, a black-and-white, featured two young women in vintage swimsuits, standing on a beach boardwalk, wearing straw hats and eating cotton candy, smiling as they posed for the camera. Samantha could pick Gran out easily. Even though this picture was taken over sixty years ago, she had just seen those deep brown, vibrant, mischievous eyes a few weeks ago. That thought brought a new batch of tears.

Samantha wished morning would come; she had a ticket for the first flight home, but time seemed to stand still. With another heavy sigh, she wondered how her dad was holding up. Being consoled by his new wife, Madison, no doubt; the thought made her stomach hurt. *Stop it Sam!* She scolded herself. Madison was nice enough. Dad seemed happy. *It just happened too quickly for me,* she reasoned. She forced herself to focus on happy thoughts and reached for another picture. This one was taken two years ago at Christmas - her mother's last.

Samantha could see the toll cancer had taken on her mother. She was pale and thin, wearing a wig that, at least in the picture, looked natural. In spite of the hardship she'd been through that year, she was showing off her broad, Julia Roberts smile. Dad had just given her a diamond tennis bracelet. She held it in her hand; it would have hurt Dad's feelings to realize her wrist was too thin to wear it.

Mom didn't care much about things; her passion was her family and her friends. But Dad always bought her a new piece of jewelry or an electronic something-or-other that she had no idea how to use. Samantha laughed out loud at the thought of her mom trying to figure out how to use her smart phone. My smart phone is smarter than me, she used to say. Her mom succumbed to cancer that following spring, Samantha started college in the fall, and her father married Madison that Christmas. *Yes, too quickly.*

This thought brought on another choking bout of tears. She knew her dad loved her mom deeply, and he was just trying to fill a void. He has a happy life with Madison, but it wasn't the love affair he had with her mom. Samantha leaned forward and wrapped her arms around her knees. Gently rocking back and forth, she let the tears come, and they came in hard sobs.

CHAPTER 5

"Mr. Blake," Madison pleaded, using her best victim voice.

"Please, call me John," the funeral director replied, obviously nervous in Madison's presence.

"John," she repeated, "my husband is so distraught, as I'm sure you can imagine. I just want to get as much handled as possible before he gets home. I want him to be able to grieve in peace without having to think about details." She paused and leaned in closer. She was beautifully built, and she knew it. "Now, Adele's wish was to be cremated and laid to rest next to her husband's ashes in the family vault. Correct?"

"Yes, that's correct. But she just died, and her son," he paused to read the name on his clipboard, "Steven Montgomery is the executor of her will. I feel it's unreasonable to move forward this quickly, without his knowledge."

Madison laid it on as thick as she knew how. "John, when my husband got the terrible news, that his mother passed, he sobbed. Do you know what it's like to hear a grown man sob?"

John hung his head; he was all too familiar with watching people grieve. He breathed in deeply as he pondered his decision. "Are you absolutely positive this is Mr. Montgomery's wish? He has no desire to view the body before cremation?"

"I'm absolutely positive." Madison reached out and gently touched John's hand as she answered.

"Okay," he felt a twinge of guilt as he gave in, "I'll take care of it right away."

"What time can I pick up her ashes?" she tried to keep her voice sullen.

John glanced at his watch. "Four o'clock?"

"I'll see you then," she said as she walked toward the door. Just as she reached for the door knob, she looked back. "Thank you, John" she said in a husky whisper. She could tell by the look on his face he was completely infatuated with her; she was counting on that to make him keep his word.

As she pulled away from the curb, she made a call.

"How's my sweetheart?" He answered the phone enthusiastically. She missed him, and the sound of his voice made her homesick.

"I pick up Adele's ashes at four."

"Good girl. I love you."

"Love you too." She hung up, turned off the disposable phone and slid it back into her bra.

CHAPTER 6

Luke McCain sat in a booth, and picked at his breakfast while he read the full page obituary of Adele Pruitt Montgomery. She was the figure-head of the very prominent Montgomery family. *Real Estate was their game,* he thought, *owned half the city, and the better half at that.* He continued to read. The article listed Adele's many committees and non-profits. It painted her as a very giving, loving, humanitarian. *Was that true?* He wondered. *Or was that too, just for the sake of appearances?* He stared at the picture of a young Adele. Mid-thirties, he'd guess. She had dark, gently curled hair, big, dark, smiling eyes, and perfect teeth flashing for the camera. She was in full riders gear. The horse was a thoroughbred, no doubt. The pair stood in a plush green field, surrounded by white fencing. The imposing mansion was visible in the distant background; it was mostly brick with white siding accents. The main portion stood three stories high, with stately columns supporting the grand front entry. On the far right, there was a single-story section that was all glass. *Perhaps a sunroom,* he thought. A bed of flowers were planted at the base of the front-facing windows. On the far left was attached, a five-car garage, with white double doors, hanging from oversized black hinges securing each stall. The long driveway had trees lining both sides. It was picture perfect. He scoffed out loud at the very thought of it. Adele had given that home to Steven several years ago and moved into a semi-independent, very upscale, assisted-living home, where the nursing staff could check on her daily, but she was free to live her life as she pleased; or so his in-depth research had told him.

"More coffee?" The waitress asked. He slid his cup to the edge of the table indicating yes, without having to actually speak. He hoped she'd get the message; he didn't want to engage in small talk. He kept his focus on the newspaper. She got the message, poured his coffee, and retreated.

He skipped to the bottom of the article, his favorite part, and he quietly read it aloud. "Adele Pruitt Montgomery is survived by her only child, Steven, her daughter-in-law, Madison and her granddaughter, Samantha." He read that last sentence again, savoring every word, allowing it to sink in. *And then there were two,* he thought to himself, laughing at the cliché.

CHAPTER 7

Former Detective Schwinn leaned back in his soft leather chair, raising his feet to rest on his antique cherry wood desk; both gifts from his want-to-be-interior-decorator wife, Miranda. She had good taste; expensive taste, the kind that exceeded his respectable police detective salary. Making the decision to go private was a no-brainer for him. The work netted a lot more money, and he was good at it. He counted on his detective background, training, contacts and, of course, honed instincts to make ends meet. He leaned back as far as the chair would allow and continued to study the case photos he'd been given. They didn't look like crime scene pics. The old lady actually looked like she was peacefully sleeping in her chair. Eighty-three years old. She had lived a good life; her financials said so. Even in death, one could see she had great hair, manicured nails, and pampered skin; this lady had taken upscale care of herself.

"Do I dare interrupt?" Miranda stood in the doorway. She held two cups of coffee and wore a sheepish grin.

"I need an interruption," he replied as he got up, reached for the coffee cup, and kissed her cheek. "Mmm. You smell … uh, good." He laughed.

"I've been working out!" she countered. "Well, actually playing tennis on the Wii, but it was a workout." This time it was her turn to laugh. "Do I really smell?"

He loved the sound of her laugh. He loved the way she threw her head back and laughed with her whole heart. He hadn't seen much of that lately. He'd been putting in too many hours. *Time to make that right,* he thought. "Wanna have a date night tonight?" he asked, returning her grin. "You know, a date? Dinner? A movie?"

"Well, I don't know," she hesitated as if considering his offer, "tell me again, what do you do for a living? I'm trying to decide if you can afford me!" This time she threw her head back as she laughed and gave him what he was looking for.

"I'll take that as a yes." He smiled at her as they fell into peaceful quiet. *She's so beautiful, inside and out,* he thought, glancing over to watch her push strands of dark auburn hair behind her ears, a sign that her playfulness had turned serious. She leaned in and squinted as she gave the pictures her full concentration.

"Tell me," she said, as she gestured toward the open file on his desk. She settled into one of the overstuffed, high-back chairs facing his desk. Miranda loved to watch her husband work. He fascinated her.

He sighed heavily, indicating he felt stumped by this case. "The police report is calling it natural causes. Her son is the sole beneficiary, and he's about to benefit big time." Rubbing the deep wrinkle in this forehead, Schwinn tried to answer the question that just didn't make sense to him. "Why is her son insisting her death was murder?" He paused to ponder the question. "Because it was," he stated the obvious. *Why?* he wondered. "It just doesn't make sense," he said, showing Miranda the file. "If the son is the sole heir, and it was a money crime, and it's always a money crime, then he wouldn't be paying me to prove it was murder." Frustrated, he stood up again and paced the room. "I like things to make sense," he said in that quiet, pondering voice of his. "I just can't make this make sense." Feeling defeated, he stopped pacing, and reclaimed his chair.

They sat in silence, sipping their coffee and staring at crime scene photos.

CHAPTER 8

Adele Pruitt Montgomery's ashes were laid to rest beside her husband's on an overcast Tuesday afternoon. It was a beautiful, peaceful affair, with the trees showing off their fall colors. Several guests stood up to say a few words and pay their last respects; they used words like amazing, vibrant, and adventurous to describe Adele.

After the service, friends and family were invited back to Steven and Madison's home. Steven, ever the techie, had a slide show hilighting his mother's life running on every television in the house. A young Adele with her husband Edmond on a fishing boat, Adele laughing, Edmond soaking wet. Adele holding her newborn son, glowing with pride. Adele wearing a poodle skirt at a costume party; Edmond standing behind her, with his rolled up jeans and cigarette pack rolled in the short sleeve of his white T-shirt, making a peace sign behind her head. Adele, Edmond, and a very young Steven posing in front of the Grand Canyon. A middle-aged Adele posing with her riding team, Adele sitting with Samantha on a blanket, outside, surrounded by stuffed animals, having a tea party. The feed just kept scrolling. There were so many pictures it seemed to never repeat.

As hired help passed through the rooms with trays of cheese and crackers, fried artichoke hearts, glazed chicken bites, and the like, guests shared hugs, condolences, stories, laughter, and tears. Steven was cordial and polite, but quietly he observed the crowd. Part of him ached to go upstairs, close the door, and mourn privately, but part of him felt like something was off. He couldn't place it, but he knew it, his instincts told him so. He continued to accept condolences as he observed the room. For a brief moment he locked eyes with Schwinn. Not a word was spoken, but they had an understanding.

Samantha quietly stood beside her father. He smiled at her as he put his forehead to hers. "Sammie," was all he could say. She was a beauty. She possessed a strong likeness to her late mother, beautiful, broad smile, long, light-brown, shiny hair, with natural streaks of blond in it, hazel, blue-green eyes, full of life. Well, usually they were full of life. Today, he had to admit, they looked a little dim. It broke his heart to see her like this. He kissed her forehead before straightening to greet and thank the next well-wisher. Samantha was going to be home from school all week. He was grateful for that. He wanted some time with her; he needed time with her. She understood his pain.

CHAPTER 9

Samantha sat in an Adirondack chair on the balcony off the family room. It was a beautiful view, overlooking the stables with lots of trees in various stages of fall coloring. She had been as polite as she could. She'd accepted condolences and smiled at stories and memories shared. Now she needed a break. She needed silence. She cursed at the sound of the French doors opening.

"Is this seat taken?" Officer Ryan gestured at the vacant Adirondack chair next to Samantha's.

"No. Please have a seat." More politeness; why couldn't she just say she needed a moment alone? Because her proper upbringing wouldn't allow such a rudeness.

"Thank you." He sat. Much to Samantha's grateful surprise, several minutes passed in total silence. They both just sat there, deep in their own thought, enjoying the beautiful view of the mansion's landscaped grounds.

"Thank you," she whispered, realizing he understood what she needed. He only nodded in return.

Several more minutes passed before it was she, once again, who broke the silence. "My grandmother was pretty amazing you know." Her gaze was fixed on the trees. "I've learned so much from her. She taught me to ride; she was a great riding instructor. She and grandfather bought me my first horse, Belle." She laughed at the name. "I was six and completely in love with the Disney cartoon, 'Beauty and the Beast.'" She brought her knees up to her chest and wrapped her arms around them as she reveled in the memory. Officer Ryan smiled but said nothing. "Her registered name is Southern Belle," she continued. "My grandmother spent hours with me, helping me overcome my fear; teaching me what Belle's mannerisms meant, showing me how to groom her."

Samantha turned to face him; shifting her focus on him. "I don't know your name," she stated as if it surprised her to realize this fact.

"Ryan. Uh, Grayson. Officer Grayson Ryan." He stumbled over his words. Why did she make him so nervous? "Call me Gray," he finally offered with a laugh.

"Gray," she repeated softly. "Nice to meet you. And, thank you again." She got up from her chair. "I need to return to our guests." She paused at the door. "Are you coming?" she questioned as she looked back at him.

FACE FRONT

"I've got to head back to the station," he said as he stood to meet her at the door. "It was nice to meet you, Samantha. Please call me if you need anything." He reached for her hand, gently squeezed it, and let it go. He made his way through the house full of mourners and out the front door; pausing for only a moment to say something to Schwinn as he passed. Samantha watched him until he was no longer in sight. Madison watched Samantha.

CHAPTER 10

Exhausted, Steven slipped into bed. His head was pounding, and he just wanted to lose himself to the darkness of sleep. Madison curled up close to him. She laid her head on his chest and gently stroked his stomach.

"Are you okay?"

"Ya, hon, I'm just tired."

"Tomorrow I've got some errands to run. I've put my life on hold this week, and I have a list of things to do as long as my arm." Her tone was matter-of-fact, and he wasn't quite sure how to take it. He reminded himself they hadn't even been married a year, and she hadn't really had time to get close to his mother. Besides, he'd appreciate some time alone with Sammie.

"Okay hon," he said with a yawn.

"When will you be going to your mother's house? You'll need to go to the bank and transfer her accounts, too."

Did she not understand that he just buried his mother today? He could feel his frustration mounting. *Let it go,* he thought to himself,

I'm not up for an argument. "Not tomorrow, hon. I need a day," was all he could reply. With that said, he rolled over and faked sleep.

Madison woke up early and slipped out of bed quietly, careful not to wake Steven. Not that she really cared if she woke him, but she had plans today, and she didn't want him asking any questions she wasn't prepared to answer. She carefully lifted his wallet off his bureau, slid his driver's license out, and placed it back exactly the way it had been. She tip toed to her closet and put the license in the envelope she already had addressed and ready to mail. *Mission accomplished,* she thought and headed for her bathroom to brush her teeth and throw her long, blond hair in a ponytail. She'd shower at the gym after her daily workout. She loved this new lifestyle. Fancy gym every morning, fancy lunches and shopping with her gal pals in the afternoons, fancy car, fancy jewelry, fancy house, fancy life. Steven really was a great catch; a genuinely good guy, the kind seen in a romantic movie; the kind she didn't think really existed. She was in too deep to try to change the plan now. *Too bad,* she thought, as she glanced down at her wedding band. Three large diamonds, equal in size, one karat each. She remembered the day Steven placed it on her finger. He told her it represented the past, present, and future. He'd pointed to the first diamond and said, "Let the past stay in the past." Then he pointed to the middle diamond,

FACE FRONT

"Let us savor each moment, always appreciating the present."
Then he moved to the third diamond; he smiled and looked into
her eyes with what she thought true love might look like, "I can't
imagine a future without you and I'm so grateful you said yes!" She
remembered the sound of them laughing together that day. It felt
so real, so natural. She almost fell for it.

Her workout was vigorous. She'd been pushing herself really
hard lately. She was in amazing shape, and she loved it. But that
wasn't her motivation today. She was trying to escape, but no
matter how fast she ran on the treadmill or how many miles she
biked, in the end she found herself staring in the mirror trying to
figure out who she'd become and realizing there simply was no
escape.

CHAPTER 11

"You sure you're okay with this?" Grayson was concerned because she seemed too quiet. "If you're not enjoying yourself, we could make an excuse and leave."

"No. I'm okay," she lied. It was her turn to bowl, so she flashed him that beautiful smile of hers and headed for the ball return to retrieve her rented ten-pound ball. She knew she needed to get out and be active, but her heart just felt so heavy all the time. It was a real effort just to be social. Besides, this was a policeman's charity tournament; her grandmother lived for charities. Samantha knew participating in this would have made her grandmother happy; the thought made her smile. "This one's for you Gran," she whispered as she rolled the ball down the alley. "Strike!" she yelled in disbelief as she turned around and gave Grayson a knuckle bump.

"Not bad for your first time."

"Not bad period," she corrected.

"You're right. Way to finish out your game." He was happy to see this sudden burst of life in her. She had holed up for over a week after the funeral, and then it took him three tries to get her to go out with him. "Are you hungry?" he asked. "A few of the guys are going to the café to get chicken wings. You up for it?"

"Uh, well…" She hesitated.

"I'm sorry, Sammie, I didn't mean to push."

"No, it's not that. I just have a lot of catching up to do with school."

"Okay, well, have you eaten anything tonight? Do you want me to hit a drive thru on the way home?"

"Actually, I'd love a pretzel." She pointed to the pretzels hanging in the snack bar window.

"One ninety-nine cent pretzel coming right up. You know, for being so high class and all, you're kind of a cheap date." He laughed and dodged her smack. Catching her arm mid swing he gently pulled her close, leaned in, and slipping his arms around her waist, they shared their first kiss.

"That was, uh, unexpected." She was smiling at him.

"I liked catching you off guard," he admitted. "When do you go back to Boston?"

"Sunday morning. I've got classes on Monday, one in particular, that I can't miss." She felt the heaviness return. She wasn't ready to leave her father and return to school, but she knew she didn't have a choice in the matter.

"Two days." He pointed out the obvious. "Would you like to do something tomorrow? We could walk around the Reedy Falls, grab some lunch?"

"Grayson, I'm sorry, I really wish I could. But I've got to spend tomorrow studying. I'm way behind." She reached out and touched his hand. "I'm not sure what this is," she admitted, "but I need a little time."

"I understand," he said, cursing himself mentally for pushing her.

"I'll call you once I'm settled back in Boston," she promised.

"Sounds good." He hoped she meant it. "Let's get you a pretzel dinner and get you home to study."

"Thanks." She hiked up on her toes and kissed his cheek.

CHAPTER 12

"Madison," Steven called down the staircase, "have you seen my driver's license? It's not in my wallet."

"What?"

"My license, I can't find it," he reiterated as he descended the stairs.

"And I'm to blame?" Her voice was a mixture of guilt and sarcasm.

"Whoa." He put his hand up to ward off her anger. "I only asked, I wasn't trying to make you feel responsible."

"Well, when's the last time you saw it?" her tone softened.

He thought for a moment. "I had to show it at the airport security when I flew home. I was distraught and not thinking clearly. Do you think I left it behind?"

"Makes sense," she agreed. She didn't look up at him, she couldn't look at him; she just continued to blend her fruit and vegetable drink. "Try calling to see if the airport has a lost and found," she suggested. "Or just go to the DMW and request a replacement. Really, Steven, it's not a big deal." She hit the blend button, drowning out any further conversation.

"I'll figure it out," Steven said over the sound, knowing she couldn't hear him and wasn't interested anyway. He headed back upstairs.

CHAPTER 13

Madison leaned back and closed her eyes. She was savoring every moment of this pampering. "Ouch!" She jerked her foot away from Gina, the pedicurist.

"Sorry, ma'am. You have big callus," Gina tried to explain, in her best broken English, why she had to be so rough.

"Gentle," Madison instructed as she slowly gave her foot back. She reached for the control and restarted the chair message.

"Is this seat taken?" A tall, dark-haired man with light brown eyes and light brown skin sat in the pedicure chair beside her.

Madison flashed him her best sultry look. "Well now, it appears it is," she answered in a low, husky purr. She was completely attracted to him, and she wasn't trying to hide it.

"Good morning Gina." He focused his attention on the pedicurist. "Busy morning, huh?"

"Very busy, Mr. Mike." Gina was grateful for the interruption.

"So, it's Mike then?" Madison asked, regaining his attention.

"Actually, Michael." He corrected as he held out his hand for her to shake.

"I'm Madi; nice to meet you." She shook his hand. "Not too often do I see a man in here." She continued. "Especially such a handsome one."

Gina rolled her eyes. "How's you wife, Mr. Mike? She come in today?"

"No, Gina, she won't be in today."

Madison gave Michael one last quick glance. "Gina, remember to use three coats of polish," she said in a huff, focusing her attention on her magazine.

Michael smiled at Gina as he reclined his chair and waited his turn. *Typical, obvious, beautiful blond,* he thought.

CHAPTER 14

His plane landed in Boston's Logan International Airport. He wasted no time making his way from the gate to the airport's center, where he found himself surrounded by shops and eateries. Searching the signs, he figured out how to catch the bus to Boston's subway system; the locals called it "The T". He was clad in blue jeans, a black pullover sweater, and black loafers, doing his best to blend in. He rode the subway's green line to the Government Center station, climbed the steps to the street, and turned right, heading for Faneuil Hall. *Samantha should be here tomorrow morning at eleven; lunch with her friend at Durgin Park, then continuing on her own to the aquarium for research on a school project,* he thought as he walked the area familiarizing himself with the details. He'd read every email and every text she'd sent or received; she was a creature of habit, and he knew her habits well. She would spend a couple of hours at the aquarium, then head back to her dorm to write her paper. Her roommate had gone home for the weekend. Tomorrow, he decided, was the perfect day for her to have a fatal accident.

Nearly four hours later, he checked himself into the Omni. He was cold, tired, and starved. He scolded himself for not bringing a heavier jacket. Boston, in the fall, could have some warm days but very cold nights. *Nothing a hot shower and some room service won't fix,* he thought.

"Will you require help with your luggage, Sir?"

"No, thank you. I travel light." He raised his right shoulder and gestured to the back pack he had hanging on it.

"Very well." The front desk clerk handed him a room key. "Elevators are to your left. Let us know if you require anything additional. Enjoy your stay," she said in one breath, without any emotion or variation in her tone.

Real sincere, he thought. He turned without saying a word and headed for his room. Once inside, he cranked up the heat and turned on the shower. He felt desperate to warm up; New England's raw, cold weather had chilled him to the bone. While he waited for the water to get hot, he called room service and ordered a lobster roll sandwich and a glass of house white. *When in Rome,* he thought as he hung up the phone and stepped into the steamy shower.

He awoke before his eight o'clock wake up call. He flicked on the television and walked over to the window of his hotel room, moving the blackout curtain just enough to peek out. *It looks like the sun is shining bright,* he observed. With the remote still in his hand, he aimed it at the television and channeled up until he found a weather station.

"Sixty-seven degrees and sunny," the tall, slender want-to-be-actress posing as a meteorologist reported. "with temperatures dropping to a low of forty-four after sunset," she continued, crossing her arms in front of her as if she suddenly felt a chill in the air.

Good deal, he thought. *I'll be on a flight home before sunset.* He picked up the phone and dialed room service. He ordered coffee and a ham and cheese omelet. He propped up the bed pillows and leaned against the headboard, once again aiming the remote at the television, and channel hopped until he found a sports station, NESN. He'd never heard of it. Two guys, Don and RemDawg, were recapping the hi-lights of the Red Sox this past season. *What kind of name is RemDawg?* He wondered. "They had a great season," he admitted aloud, although he wasn't a fan.

When his disposable cell phone rang, he clicked off the television and answered on the second ring. "Good morning, gorgeous."

"Somebody is in a great mood." Madison loved hearing him so happy.

"Our plan is coming together. I'm content."

"I trust your trip went well, then?"

"Perfect. I've got it all worked out. Samantha will be dead in about..." He paused to glance at his Movado watch on the night table, a gift from his daughter. "Six hours; give or take, depending on how much time she spends at the aquarium."

"Good."

"Even better, we can probably file a lawsuit against the school for their faulty wiring that cost our beloved daughter her life." He was laughing at his own quick-witted observation. "Just what we need, more money."

"Speaking of money." She changed the subject. "I opened that special account yesterday. I did it exactly as you instructed."

"That's my girl. I'll start transferring the funds as soon as I get back. I'll do it in small increments, nothing too obvious."

"Okay, sounds good. I'll let you go; you've got a very full day ahead of you. Send me a text so I know It's done."

"Will do. You're the love of my life, you know."

"I know. Love you too." She hung up and slipped the disposable phone back into her bra.

CHAPTER 15

Samantha trotted down the stairs at Government Center on her way to Durgin Park Restaurant. She could see Quincy Market in the distance. She was hungry and looking forward to lunch with her old roommate, Megan. With the sun beating down on her face and the air feeling just a bit crisp, she was enjoying the moment.

"Sammie." She turned when she heard her name called. Megan was rushing down the stairs behind her. "Wait up!" Megan called out.

"I miss you," Samantha said to her friend, giving her a quick hug. "How's life after school?"

"It's good. I was offered a position in New York!" She blurted out, excited to share her news.

"Wow! That's your dream! Megan, I'm so happy for you." She hugged her friend again as they entered the restaurant.

"Okay, your turn. Spill it," Megan demanded as they settled into their booth.

"Spill what?" Samantha tried to sound innocent.

"You dropped a hint in your text about a new guy, I believe you called him Gray."

"No mixing words with you." Samantha was smiling at her friend.

"What'll you have?" the nasty-tempered waitress asked in her thick Boston accent, as she approached their table, pad out, pen in hand, in a rush and not interested in small talk or questions. This was the famous behavior of the mean Durgin Park staff, and the patrons loved it.

"Broiled scallops and a Coke." Samantha answered as quickly as she could.

"Lobster ravioli and ice water," Megan chimed in. "Oh, and could I please have lemon in my water?" The waitress scoffed at her last request and walked away without a word.

"Okay, okay, details," Samantha continued. "Well, his name is Grayson, and I met him about five weeks ago, when I went home. He's a cop. He…"

"A cop!" Megan interrupted her.

"Yes, a cop."

"Oooohhh, Grandmother would not approve of that," Megan pointed out and instantly regretted it when she saw the happiness on Samantha's face fade. "Sammie, I'm sorry. I was just playing, and I didn't think before I said it."

"I know. No worries. I just miss her, you know?"

"I know." Megan reached over and touched Samantha's hand. "I'm really sorry."

"I'm okay," Samantha reassured her friend.

"Back to Grayson," Megan prompted desperately trying to snap Samantha out of the sudden sad state she'd thrown her into.

"Really, there isn't much to tell. We had a date while I was home. And we've talked on the phone almost nightly for the past month. I really like him. He's sweet and funny."

Megan leaned back in her chair and crossed her arms. "I've never seen you like this. This guy has really caught your interest," she observed.

"Coke." The waitress set the glass down in front of Samantha. "Ice watah with leeeeemon," she said, with sarcasm, setting the small bowl of sliced lemon down hard in front of Megan. The girls laughed as the waitress headed back to the kitchen.

"When do you move to New York?" Samantha asked, taking a sip of her soda, trying to change the subject.

"By the end of the month."

"That's quick."

"I know, but I'm ready."

"Scallops and lobstah rav," the waitress interrupted again, setting the lunch plates on the table. She didn't wait for a response or to see if they needed anything additional before making her retreat.

"Want company at the aquarium?" Megan asked, biting into her lunch.

"Really? Don't you have packing to do?"

"Honestly, I'm ready. Besides, we may not get too many opportunities to hang out together with me moving and all."

"My roommate has gone home for the weekend. If you want, you can spend the night at the dorm with me. We can order pizza and watch a sappy girl movie."

"Sounds good."

After lunch, the girls headed to the aquarium. Samantha pulled a pad of paper and a camera out of her backpack. "You take pictures, I'll take notes." The two girls walked around the aquarium, chatting about old times and current events, thoroughly enjoying each other's company. They finished their task in about an hour and headed for the subway.

"What are you doing?" Megan asked as she watched Samantha's fingers rapidly move over the keyboard of her cell phone.

"I'm texting the girls, you know, Brooke, Dani, and Jessica. I'll have them meet us at my dorm. We'll give you a proper send off." She smiled at Megan, pleased with her plan.

It didn't take long before Samantha and Megan were settling into Samantha's dorm room. "What time are the girls getting here?" Megan asked.

"In about twenty minutes, maybe less." She pulled the camera out of her backpack and plugged it in the side of her computer. "I'm just going to download the aquarium pictures while we wait." The computer was dead. "What the heck?" Samantha tried pushing the power button again.

"It's unplugged." Megan pointed to the wall plug, then bent down to plug the computer back in.

"Megan!" Samantha screamed as she watched in stunned horror. Megan's body shook silently. Samantha could hear a low buzzing sound, and she could actually smell the electrical outlet burning. Acting on instinct, she kicked her friend hard knocking them both to the ground, free of the current. She felt the electricity shoot up her leg. Samantha struggled to get up. She was disoriented and she felt a painful tingle in her teeth. She grabbed her cell phone and dialed 9-1-1. Megan's limp body was white as a sheet and unresponsive. Samantha desperately tried to revive her while she waited for the ambulance to arrive, but Megan was pronounced dead at the scene.

"Miss Montgomery." The paramedic approached Samantha. "I'm afraid I'm going to have to insist you allow us to take you to the hospital."

"I'm fine." The words came out in a sob. She was surrounded by her friends; they were huddled together, sitting on Samantha's bed, in shock.

"Miss Montgomery." The paramedic tried to reason with her. "What you were hit with is equivalent to a taser current. I'm sure you are fine, but I must insist we take you in for a complete evaluation. Most likely they will release you in a couple hours."

Samantha's cell phone rang, and she answered it immediately when she saw her father's number on the caller I.D. "Daddy!" she cried.

"I know, Sammie." His heart broke for her. He hated that he couldn't get to her fast enough. "I'm on my way to the airport, I've booked a flight," he reassured her. "I land at Logan tonight at eleven-twenty. I'm going to catch a taxi and go straight to the hospital to pick you up."

"Dad, I'm okay, I don't need to go to the hospital. I'm just a little shook up, but I'm not hurt."

"Samantha, I will meet you at the hospital. I believe you, but I want to be sure."

"Okay," she conceded.

"Okay," Steven confirmed. "I'll pick you up tonight, and we'll fly home together tomorrow morning."

"But I have finals in two weeks. I was planning to come home for Christmas, after finals."

He knew she was in denial, or perhaps even shock. She couldn't possibly be worried about finals when she just witnessed her friend die. "Sammie. You just lost one of your friends in a horrible accident, and you got quite an electric jolt in the process. You need to get checked out by a doctor, then you need to come home with me to recover. I will call your professors, and we'll try to work something out." His tone was clear; he was not giving her an option.

"Okay, Dad. I'll see you tonight." She touched the end button on her cell phone and turned her attention to her friends, still huddled together. "Which one of you called my dad?"

"Me," Brooke quietly confessed.

"Thank you," Samantha said, knowing her friend had done it for her own good. "I'm ready to go to the hospital with you," She said to the paramedic.

CHAPTER 16

"Don't panic; I'll come up with another plan." He was desperately trying to console her. He couldn't let her fall apart on him now.

"Samantha can't just have another accident! People aren't going to believe it's a coincidence!" She was desperately trying to regain her composure. "They'll notice something's not right!"

"Samantha didn't have an accident in the dorm; her friend did," he reminded her, using his most gentle sounding voice. "The police think it was faulty wiring in that old building. Even the newspaper reported it as a most unfortunate and terrible mishap. Nobody is noticing anything."

"We're running out of time," she protested.

"We'll make the time schedule," he promised.

"You're right," she agreed with a dramatic exhale.

"I know you're tired of living this lie, but hang in there, my sweetheart, it will be over soon. We'll stick to our time schedule for now. Let me come up with another plan to get Samantha out of our way." His voice was soothing, reassuring.

"Okay. When do we talk again?"

"Three days, same time? Will that work for you? Can you get away?"

"Of course I can." Her voice filled with a renewed confidence. "I love you." She hung up, not waiting for him to reply.

CHAPTER 17

The phone ringing was a welcomed interruption. It had been almost two months, and Steven still couldn't focus on anything, especially work.

"Good morning Steve." The voice on the line was breaking up; bad cell reception. "This is Luke Boyd. We talked a few months ago regarding a luxury housing project in Las Vegas."

"Yes. Luke. Yes, I'm so sorry I didn't get back in touch with you. I've had a personal loss recently, and I'm afraid I just needed to put work on hold for a bit."

"I read about your mother passing in the paper. I'm very sorry for your loss." The construction noise in the background disguised his all-business, insincere tone.

"Thank you. I'm afraid I haven't had a chance to look at the specs you sent me. But I will do that today; I need to dive back into things. Can you give me until Friday?"

"Absolutely; I'll give you a call Friday morning. Steve, I'd really like to get you out here to look at the project. Of course, I will pick up all the expenses. I think this is a partnership that will be quite lucrative for both of us. Will you consider making the trip?"

"I'll consider it. Speak with you Friday." He hung up the phone and reached for his laptop. He googled Luke Boyd and when several hundred appeared, he realized that the effort was moot.

CHAPTER 18

Schwinn sat at his dining room table with pictures spread out in front of him. He had been tailing the Montgomery Three as he'd nicknamed them: Steven, Madison and Samantha. Follow the money, was his motto. "Follow the money," he said aloud, repeatedly. And, well, in this case the money just wasn't making sense.

Steven was wealthy in his own right, quite the real estate mogul. In addition, Adele had turned a large portion of her real estate holdings over to him long before her passing. He was worth roughly three times as much as she. Not to mention, Steven had hired him, which made him the least likely candidate. But, Schwinn wasn't ruling him out yet; he'd seen this scenario before. After all, Steven was the sole beneficiary.

Madison was already enjoying the benefit of Steven's money; that was obvious by the car she drove, the clothes she wore, and the way she spent. And she had a rock-solid alibi; she was having dinner at Banchero's with five other women, girls' night out while her husband was out of town. Dinner lasted over two hours and then she caught a movie with two of the girls she'd dined with;

this accounted for another two plus hours. They drove from the restaurant to the theater in one car, and their proximity to the victim's house was at least forty minutes distance. Detective Schwinn let out a heavy sigh. He was frustrated; he couldn't seem to connect the dots. "Well, Madison, you're smart. I'll give you that." He stared at a photo of Madison exiting a salon. He'd taken it a few days ago, from a distance, while tailing her. He could see how she landed the prominent Steven Montgomery; she was the complete package. "How'd you do it, girl?" he asked her photo. "Did you hire out the job? Why? You've got all the money you'll ever want or need."

He scribbled the word "dig" on a post-it note and stuck it to Madison's photo. It was a reminder to him that he didn't know much about Madison's past. He probably should remedy that.

Samantha would inherit it all but not until her father passed. Besides, she didn't seem to want for anything. She had looked so pale and broken at Adele's funeral; it was obvious she had taken her grandmother's passing very hard. And, of course, she was a couple thousand miles away at school. "Distance," he said aloud, knowing distance and witnesses were always the best alibis.

"Follow the money," he repeated with another heavy sigh. He pulled his cell phone out of his pocket and hit speed dial button four. Roger was his ex-partner and best friend. He needed a new set of eyes and maybe some unpublished case facts.

"Talk to me, Schwinn," Roger was always so up! It could be annoying in long increments, like a full day of riding in a police car.

"I need you, Rog. I need fresh eyes, a fresh perspective. I'm willing to pay the stiff price of burgers and beer." He laughed, but it came out tense and exposed his true frustration.

"You got it. I'll swing by your house at eighteen hundred. Have the burgers on the grill, and the beer on ice."

"Copy. My house. Eighteen hundred," he repeated back to him. Old habits die hard.

He hung up the phone and began to organize the photos in a timeline, starting with the obituary photo of Adele that appeared in the paper. She was a raven beauty. Even the low-quality newspaper photo showed off her flawless tanned skin and piercing dark eyes. He went back, adding the facts he'd obtained so far, barely legible, written in what his wife called 'chicken scratch' on post-it notes.

CHAPTER 19

Samantha was enjoying herself. She was laughing out loud. The sound seemed foreign to her ears. It had been a while since she really laughed.

"Thank you Gray," she said smiling at Grayson. "This is a much needed distraction."

"Well, I'm glad you came home for Christmas vacation. The way you kept hem-hawing, I really thought you were going to back out." He took another bite of his pizza.

She didn't tell him about Megan's accident in her dorm or that her father insisted she come home; she didn't feel the need to share it. "I just wasn't sure I had it in me to deal with Madison. She's so gushy and clingy with my dad. It actually makes me sick to my stomach. You know she's only eight years older than me." She felt her mood shift. "Seventeen years younger than my dad."

"That bothers you?" It was as much an observation as a question.

"No. Actually, I think what bothers me is that my mom had barely passed and Madison swooped in so fast. Trying to figure it out makes my head spin." She focused on her long, polished nails, gently rubbing little circle patterns over them. "My mom, dad, and I used to be so tight-knit; 'the three-strand chord,' mom used to say." She smiled at the memory of her mother. "When I try to do things with Dad and Madison, I feel like the third wheel; odd man out." She glanced up to look Gray in the eyes. "They even look alike!" she said, staring at Gray for confirmation. "They both have those pale blue eyes." She tried to explain. "Mom used to call them 'husky eyes.'" She lowered her head again. "Sometimes I feel like I'm the step," she paused trying to search for the right words, "and Madison is blood." She couldn't explain herself properly, and it was frustrating her to try.

He reached for her hand and gently rubbed his thumb across the top as he held it. He could see her pain and wanted to fix it, but he knew he couldn't. His heart ached to rescue her. He was falling in love with her. Crazy, he told himself. He'd only seen her a half dozen times, but they'd talked on the phone almost nightly for the past couple of months.

"You know, if Gran were alive, she wouldn't approve of me dating you." She played with him, changing the subject and lightening the mood. "She was big on appearances. She would have expected me to date someone who could trace their bloodline back to the Mayflower." She laughed.

"Well, I may be country, but I can assure you my family tree does have branches!" he pointed out. She threw her head back and laughed from her heart. It pleased him.

"Would you like to go riding?" She actually sounded happy.

"I think...uh, yes. But be warned, I don't know much about riding." He knew nothing about riding. He'd never actually been on a horse.

"I can teach you. It'll be fun. Truuust me." She stretched out the word and gave him her best mischievous smile. She reached over and took another piece of pizza from the tray. She was enjoying his company. And perhaps, she was finally starting to heal.

CHAPTER 20

Detective Roger Donovan parked in front of his former partner's house. He grabbed the file and the six-pack and headed for the door. Miranda answered it before he could even knock. She threw her arms around him, kissed his cheek, and scolded him for being such a stranger. He loved her; she was family. She pointed him to the dining room and promptly got out of his way. Despite appearances, she knew this was business.

"If this is what retirement looks like, I want no part of it," Roger said as he entered the dining room. There were photos, files, and post-it notes everywhere. But Roger recognized the organized chaos.

"I want to pin it on the son," Schwinn replied, jumping right into business. "It makes sense to pin it on him. But he has an airtight, rock solid alibi. He was over two thousand miles away on a business trip, with lots of witnesses and a used airline ticket. And when he got the news, it took him three flights and with weather delays and misconnections, nearly eighteen hours to get home."

"Not to mention, he hired you in the first place," Roger added.

"C'mon, Rog. You know that doesn't make him innocent," Schwinn protested.

"Hear me." Roger moved in closer as he spoke. "It was already ruled natural causes. It's a closed case as far as the department is concerned. It doesn't make sense for the son to stir the pot. This isn't some street punk we're dealing with, who doesn't know when to shut up. This is a smart, business savvy, entrepreneur." He paused for a brief moment and then continued. "Besides, you saw how distraught he was at her funeral. That wasn't guilt; that was heavy, deeply-felt loss."

Schwinn nodded his head. He knew Roger was right. "You see the pics." He gestured toward the crime scene photos he had spread out on the dining room table. "The way the knitting needles were under the chair. If she had dropped them, they would have been beside the chair, not under it. And her lipstick was smeared. Not like 'she just had a snack smeared', but like something pressed against her lips and moved in an upward motion!" Schwinn stood up, his voice rising with excitement. "I wish we could have done an autopsy. I'll bet it would have proved she was suffocated."

"I'm not denying she was murdered," Roger's voice was especially low and calm; he was trying to help his friend settle down. "I've studied the pics and read the file; I wish we had enough to have kept it an open case because, absolutely, I agree, she was murdered. But what I'm saying is, I think we need to get off the son for a moment and see who else may have wanted Adele Montgomery to meet her maker. Let's talk about Madison."

"No. Her alibi checks out. No way that many women could lie and be in agreement." Schwinn leaned back and stretched his arms behind his head. "I have to admit though, I like her for the job. She reaps benefits and has no real attachment or loss. Plus, it burns me that she cremated the body so fast; it's suspicious."

"Suspicious behavior, yes," Roger agreed. "But it doesn't make her a murderer." He leaned over and picked up the manila file with Madison's name on it. He read aloud. "Born Madison Ann McCain; March twenty-fifth, nineteen eighty-six; Las Vegas, Nevada to Luke McCain, aged seventeen, and Judy Olsen, also seventeen, not married." He flipped a page and continued. "High school graduate, some college, no degree. Beeeauuuty queen." He said with sarcasm. "Miss Vegas Regional." He looked at Schwinn over the folder he was holding. "What's a Miss Regional?" he asked, laughing and shaking his head. He closed the file and tossed it back on the table. "No arrest record. She was working as a flight attendant when she landed the prominent Steven Montgomery, which means she passed the FAA required ten year background check. She's clean." He tossed the file back down on the table.

"Samantha Montgomery." He said, picking up her file folder. "She was away at school; UMass, Boston. And, like her father, she couldn't get home until the next day due to lousy flight schedules and delays." He rubbed his chin as he read her file. "She had nothing to gain," he conceded. "She inherits from her father, and Adele would naturally pass long before him anyway. If she was the doer it would make a lot more sense for her to kill her father and ride out her grandmother's life, knowing it would be a lot less time to wait, and she would have significantly cut out Madison in the process." He tossed Samantha's file back on the table on top of Madison's.

"Who else we got?" Roger asked, full of energy and ready to solve this case. "Who else benefits? Who else may have been holding a grudge?"

Schwinn shrugged his shoulders, gesturing to all the evidence he had spread out on the dining room table, well aware that it didn't add up to much.

The two men sat in silence, sifting through files searching for possible motives. They combed through every aspect of Adele's life: her business partners, her fund-raisers and charities, her friendships and acquaintances. They found nothing.

"You boys hungry?" Miranda asked from the kitchen. "You've been at it for a couple hours now, and I know a break would do you some good." She set the kitchen table. She didn't hear a reply, but she could hear movement. She opened the oven door and pulled out a roast, with potatoes, carrots, broccoli, summer squash, and zucchini surrounding it. The delicious smell filled the air. Almost like magic, the men appeared in the kitchen. She knew this would get them.

"Wow, Miranda, this smells great. I thought we were just having burgers. Wow," Roger repeated. "This is really great."

"I thought you may appreciate something a little better than burgers," she replied as she motioned him to sit down.

"Thank you," her husband whispered in her ear as he kissed her cheek. He knew Roger, recently divorced, didn't get many home-cooked meals; this obviously meant a lot to him.

"Save room for ice cream," Miranda told Roger. "Edy's Butter Pecan still your favorite?" She smiled at him.

"Now you're just plain spoiling me!" He laughed.

Two helpings of roast beef, one glass of wine, and a dish of ice cream later, Roger was at the front door, saying good night and thanking them again for dinner. He had a pad of notes and two files tucked under his arm; homework.

"Thanks, brother." Schwinn said as he patted Roger's shoulder. "See you Friday."

"Friday," Roger confirmed and headed down the steps to his car.

CHAPTER 21

Grayson pulled onto the long driveway that led to the Montgomery mansion. He passed through the grand arched entry and passed the rows of Italian cypress trees that lined both sides of the drive. *This place is awesome,* he thought, feeling very much out of his league. Samantha was sitting on her horse to the left of the house, waiving at him to pull around to the back where the stables were. He parked in front of the barn and got out of his car. He glanced down and gave himself a quick survey, a sweatshirt, blue jeans, and boots; nothing fancy. He didn't own riding gear. He watched her gallop towards him, her long hair blowing in the wind, sharing that beautiful smile of hers. For a moment, he forgot he was afraid. "Good morning, beautiful."

"Good morning back." She played with him. "Are you ready to ride?"

"Remember you need to go easy on me." He felt his fear return and gave up trying to hide it.

"Well, let me show you some basics, and then we'll walk a trail."

"Sounds like a plan."

She reached her arm down to him. "Put your left foot in the stirrup, she instructed. "Then swing your right leg over."

He obliged. "Okay, that was easy."

"Put your arms around me."

"Now we're getting somewhere," he joked.

She gave Belle a gentle nudge with her heels, and the horse began to walk. Grayson squeezed Samantha tighter. "We're good," she reassured him. "This is easy right."

"Uh-huh." He was sweating.

"I was going to saddle up Rocket for you, but I'm wondering if you would rather just ride double on Belle with me."

"Double." He paused for a second as the horse made a funny noise through her nostrils. "Definitely double," he confirmed.

"Double it is then. We're just going to walk her by the water trough and give her a little drink before we hit the trail."

"I could use a drink right about now," Grayson joked.

As Belle lowered her head to drink, Samantha felt Grayson's grip around her waist tighten. "Would you like to have dinner with us tonight?" She was trying to make casual conversation with him to relax him. "We're having a low country boil and I'd like you to meet my father."

"I've met your father." His voice was strained.

"I mean, really meet him."

"I'd love that, Sam. Thanks for inviting me, but what's a low country boil?" He relaxed his grip.

"You've never had a low country boil?"

"No, ma'am."

"Well, it's a variety of seafood, shell-fish, lobster, crab, and shrimp mixed with potatoes, corn and onion, boiled in a pot. When it's good and tender, and the water has boiled down, they dump the pot on the table, and you just scoop a portion out of it. It's sloppy and delicious. You'll love it."

"Sounds great."

Belle raised one of her front legs, and Grayson immediately tightened his grip again. Samantha laughed. "She's relaxed," she tried to explain. "That's how horses rest." She gently stroked the side of her horse's neck. "Okay, Miss Belle," she told her horse. "That's enough for now." She tugged the reins to the right, and her horse followed her lead. They gently walked the first half mile or so enjoying the scenery and each other. "Would you like to try trotting?" Samantha asked.

"What's trotting?" Grayson asked, making Samantha laugh again.

"Let's try it, and if it scares you, we'll stop." She gave Belle another gentle nudge with her heels and made a funny noise in her cheek, and Belle picked up the pace.

"And we're trotting," Grayson said trying to figure out if he liked it or not. He had to admit, he preferred to move a little faster, but the pounding that came with trotting was actually a little painful. "What other speeds do you have?" he asked.

"Hold on," Samantha called back. She gave Belle another heel nudge and cheek prompt and Belle broke into a gentle, gliding run. Her stride was long and graceful. No more pounding. It was actually peaceful. Now Grayson was enjoying himself.

It took them less than fifteen minutes of an easy run with Southern Belle to reach the back end of the Montgomery property. Along this edge flowed a creek; Samantha slowed her horse to a walking pace as they approached it. "I'm going to let her have another drink." When they got near the water, Samantha let Belle's reins rest gently on her saddle's horn. Belle lowered her head to drink; the movement no longer scared Grayson.

"Tell me about your mom."

"My mom? Well, um." She hesitated for a moment; she didn't know where to start. "Well, my mom was a beautiful lady, inside and out. And I loved the sound of her voice." She paused for a moment, remembering the sound of Kate's voice. "When I was little, she would wrap me in her arms to read me a story, and she would put such drama in the sound of the character's voices. She was great like that." Samantha twisted her body in the saddle to face Grayson. "She was a nurse. When she and my dad first got married, they traveled with missionary groups to third world countries. My dad would help build hospital facilities and orphanages, and my mom would assist the medical staff. I've seen pictures; my dad has photo albums in his study. I used to pull them out and tease them about their funny hair styles and clothes from more than twenty years ago, but now when I look at the pictures, I see the incredible work they did."

"Is that something you aspire to do someday?"

"My mom and dad quit traveling like that when they learned she was pregnant with me. I think it was somewhat dangerous and they didn't want to take any chances. After I was born, mom decided not to go back to work, but instead she volunteered a couple days a week, giving medical treatment in homeless shelters downtown. I think that's more along the lines of what I want to do."

"A very worthy cause, Miss Montgomery," Grayson observed. He felt proud of Samantha, proud of her loving, giving heart.

Samantha reached for Belle's reins and gave her a gentle tug; Belle shook her head back and forth to show her disapproval as she stepped back away from the creek. After a couple hours of walking on trails and running through fields, they decided to head back to the barn. Samantha halted Belle just in front of the barn gates. "Whoa, girl. Steady." When the horse was settled, she turned her attention to Grayson. "Go ahead and slide off her left side. Hold my arm for balance." He did. Samantha jumped down beside him. She pulled Belle's reins to the front of the horses head and led her into the barn. Grayson followed behind her, walking as if he were still straddling the horse. Samantha laughed again; she enjoyed his company. "Okay, we need to brush her down. Be serious." She gave him a playful smack.

"I am being serious," he countered. "My legs are ruined."

Samantha laughed even louder. "Maybe a little sore, but most definitely not ruined!"

"Okay, when you brush her, use long strokes, front to back." She was trying to be serious, but she couldn't stop laughing at him. "Gray, pay attention; this is important."

"Okay."

"When you move to the other side, keep your hand on her, so she feels you the whole time you move around her; otherwise you could startle her."

"Got it; constant contact so I don't startle her. Wait. What happens if I startle her?"

"She'll kick you."

"Okay, definitely keep constant contact and do not, under any circumstances, startle the horse."

Samantha reached into the pocket of her coat and pulled out a couple of carrots. "Want to give her a treat?"

"Oh, I thought those were for me."

"One for you, one for Belle." She laughed and handed him a carrot. "Watch me." She held the carrot in the palm of her hand and offered it to Belle. "Keep your palm flat so she doesn't accidentally bite you."

"You are pushing me way out of my comfort zone today," he said as he offered his flat palm to Belle. As she gently took the carrot from him, he reached up to pet the side of her long face. He loved every minute of this.

"Thank you Sam." He wiped his hand on his jeans and looked at Samantha. "Today was an awesome day. Thank you." He leaned in and kissed her. "I'm going to head home to shower. What time do you want me to come back for dinner?"

"Four would be good; and come around back, we'll have a tent and tables set up out here. Low country boil is best served outside."

"It's a little cool for outdoor dining, don't you think?"

"We usually don't do this sort of thing until spring, but Madison is insisting on doing it now." She rolled her eyes. "Maybe she isn't planning to stick around until spring." She smiled up at Grayson, then quickly added, "Sorry, that wasn't very nice to say."

"Don't let her get to you, Sammie. Just kill her with kindness. Eventually you two will find common ground."

"We've rented tents and outdoor heaters." She tried to steer the conversation back to the subject of dinner. "So, it'll be okay."

"Sounds great. Four o'clock, around back," he confirmed as he leaned down and kissed her good-bye. "See you then, beautiful."

CHAPTER 22

Steven watched Madison through the window of his study. He could see her arms flailing about as she instructed the staff to set up tents, outdoor heaters, and the like. He knew he should go outside and rescue them, but then who would rescue him? He dreaded dealing with this side of Madison. She could become completely out of control when she didn't get her way. He quietly opened the window, just a fraction, to try to eavesdrop on the conversation. Madison's voice was at an alarming high pitch. This was bad. He leaned closer to the window, trying to catch what she was saying. Something about incompetent, worthless. *Uh-oh*, he thought, and raced down the stairs and out the back door. He needed to intervene before the entire staff, not just the ones hired specifically for this party, walked off the job. When the door opened suddenly, and Steven came out in a rush, Madison turned to him and immediately gushed with tears.

"Steven, they're trying to sabotage my affair!" She rushed into his arms.

"Sweetheart, I'm sure they're not doing it on purpose." He held her awkwardly and gently patted her back. He looked up at the staff with a sincere look of sympathy for them. "Why don't you go inside, and let me handle this?" he suggested.

She pulled away from his embrace. "Do you think you can?" she questioned.

Was she serious? He thought. "Yes, I'm sure I can," he replied, biting his tongue.

She glanced over her shoulder, giving the staff one final look of disapproval, and headed for the house.

"Okay, what have we got here?" Steven asked the staff, joining with them in a team huddle. They went over the set up instructions Madison had given them, and in less than an hour they were finished. "Great job, everybody," Steven called out as he surveyed the job. "It looks perfect," he added sharing high-fives with his staff.

CHAPTER 23

For the second time today, Grayson found himself admiring the pure splendor of the Montgomery Mansion's grounds. He pulled around back, as instructed, and parked at the far end near the barn, trying and failing to blend with the high end cars parked along the edge of the white fence. In the distance he could see the tops of white party tents set up in a row. *What's the music?* He wondered, not recognizing the sound. As he rounded the barn and got the full view of what he thought was going to be a little backyard dinner; he was shocked. Long tables, that seemed to go on forever, were placed end to end underneath the rows of tents. Clear twinkle lights hung from the tents ceiling supports. Fine china and silver-rimmed wine glasses, designated a place at the table for each guest; service for sixty, Grayson guessed. In the corner a live band played. He didn't recognize the music. *Maybe a local band playing some of their own stuff,* he thought. A portable, wooden dance floor, with pots of flowers and candles lining the edges, was set up near the band. He had been to weddings that weren't this elaborate.

Feeling completely out of place, Grayson glanced down at his outfit of choice, jeans and a button down shirt.

"You're two minutes late." Samantha played with him as she wrapped her arms around his neck and gave him a quick kiss.

"I thought this was a casual, I believe you said, 'sloppy' affair."

"You look great; don't worry about it." She tugged at his arm. "Let me introduce you."

Grayson followed Samantha's lead. He met Mayor Chapin and a couple of other political figures, along with several business owners and entrepreneurs. Christopher Hayden, owner of Hayden's Place restaurant, gave him a business card and invited him to bring Samantha for dinner on the house. "What's that?" Grayson asked Samantha when he heard a chime.

"It's time to take our seat; dinner is ready to be served." She led Grayson to the end of the first table where they would be sitting with Mayor and Mrs. Chapin, Steven, and Madison.

The waiters filed out in a row of ten, all wearing black pants and white shirts with red ties. Each carried a steaming pot of the low country boil Samantha had described; it was a sight to see. Like synchronized swimmers, they poured their pots onto the tables in unison. Grayson watched in awe as the middle of each table held a mound of lobster, crab legs, shrimp, scallops, potatoes, and corn.

"Wow," he whispered to Samantha. "This is crazy; I've never seen anything like this." He reached for his bib and tied it around his neck. "Thank you for inviting me."

"You're welcome."

"What's the occasion, anyway?"

"No occasion; just Madison showing off." She tilted her head and smiled at him. "Usually, in years past, when we have one of these it's about a dozen people and a couple of staff." She glanced around at the grandeur. "This is just Madison being Madison."

"Well, let's enjoy it to the fullest; after dinner, may I have the first dance?"

"You may."

CHAPTER 24

"Steven's plane was delayed over an hour, but he's on his way now."
Madison spoke into the disposable cell phone.

"I know. He called me. I'm ready for him." His voice was deep
and serious. None of the playfulness she was used to hearing when
he spoke with her. "His trip was scheduled for three days, right?"

"Right," she confirmed.

"When is your flight?"

"Tomorrow morning. Six o'clock"

"I'll park your car in the garage, on the roof-top, as close to the
elevator as I can get. Three days should be enough time for you to
take care of the arrangements." He reasoned. "I'll have everything
ready when you arrive so you won't waste any time."

"Okay. I booked our return flight on Thursday afternoon at three-
fifteen. I'll plan to pick you up at the Crown on my way to the airport."

"Perfect. I miss you baby; I'm looking forward to seeing you
tomorrow."

"Tomorrow," she repeated, then broke the connection and
placed the disposable cell phone back into her bra.

CHAPTER 25

"Are you sure you don't want a ride to the airport?" Samantha asked, trying to befriend this woman who was in her life now whether she liked it or not.

"No, I've already made arrangements, but thanks anyway." Madison replied.

"You're sure I can drive your Mercedes while you're gone? I don't mind taking the Jeep."

"Don't be silly. The Jeep is drafty. It's hard to stay warm in it this time of year. I don't mind you driving my car. You're responsible, right?" She smiled at Samantha.

"Of course." Samantha stood in the doorway and watched Madison pack. "Dad's going to love that you surprised him like this." Madison smiled but didn't answer. "Well, I'll leave you alone. I'm going to call it a night, get to bed early. I've got a long list of errands tomorrow. You know, gearing up to go back to school." She was at a loss for words. "And perhaps a special date." She let her final statement hang in the air a few seconds, hoping Madison would show some interest. Getting no response, she turned and headed back to her room. *So much for friendship,* she thought. *I have absolutely nothing in common with her.*

"I've got a special date for you too." Madison whispered to herself. She couldn't wait to get Samantha out of the way. Steven was easy to manipulate. But Samantha, no, she was sharp, questioned everything and always in the way.

CHAPTER 26

Steven marveled at the architecture of Las Vegas as his plane descended upon the twenty-four hour city that never sleeps. He felt the wheels touch ground and was relieved to be almost there. He was tired. He was looking forward to a hot shower, a good meal, and a comfortable bed. With a twinge of guilt, he admitted to himself that he was grateful to get a break from Madison. *Things have been tense between us lately,* he thought. *She's always on edge.* For the first time in their marriage, Steven entertained the thought that maybe he'd moved too quickly marrying Madison; he still felt the void of losing Kate.

"Are you getting off here?" the elderly gentleman sitting in the window seat of Steven's row asked. "Or are you continuing on to Oakland? I need to get off here." He gestured for Steven to move from his aisle seat to let him pass.

"Oh, sorry," Steven replied, snapping back to reality. "Yes, I'm off here, too." He jumped to his feet, trying to wedge himself into an already crowded narrow airplane aisle. The man seemed annoyed; Steven couldn't figure out why. He couldn't move any faster; actually, he couldn't move at all. He could see from the man's window, that they were still pulling up the jetbridge. *Let it go,* he told himself as he smiled at the elderly man, who did not return the kind gesture. Within minutes the plane emptied into the Las Vegas terminal. Steven slipped his garment bag strap over his head and pushed the bag under his right arm, securing it, hands free, close to his body. He reached for his cell phone in his shirt pocket and dialed Madison to let her know he'd landed. When her voicemail picked up, he opted not to leave a message. He bypassed the baggage claim and headed straight for the front door. As he neared the door, he saw the sign bearing his name. "Welcome Steven Montgomery" was all it read.

"I'm Steven Montgomery," he said to the man holding the sign. *What an odd looking man,* he thought. *Face glossy, like perhaps he'd been in a fire and, was he wearing a wig?* Steven thought, trying not to stare.

"I've got your car, sir. I'm instructed to take you to Mr. Boyd's home."

"Okay. Thank you," Steven replied, disappointed to hear there would be a stop along the way to his hotel. He gestured for the driver to lead the way. *I have a driver,* he grinned at the thought.

FACE FRONT

Means I don't have to be the driver, he concluded as he and the driver made their way to the reserved-for-limo-only curb parking.

The driver pushed a button on his key and released the truck lock with a popping sound. Steven handed him his garment bag. When the driver reached for Steven's briefcase, Steven was ready to protest, but decided he was too tired to look at work right now anyway, so what difference did it make? When the driver opened the limo door, Steven slid inside and sank into the luxury of the back seat. He could fall asleep so easily, but he fought the urge.

"It's approximately forty minutes to Mr. Boyd's estate." The driver spoke to him through the window that divided the cab from the cabin. "I've stocked the mini bar for you. Please help yourself."

"Thank you," Steven replied. *What is it about this driver?* Steven thought. *He is so polite and attentive, but something is off.* He couldn't quite place it.

As Steven reached for a bottled water, the driver closed the partition window. Steven leaned back and sipped the water he'd poured over ice with a wedge of lemon and lime, just the way he liked it. He was relaxed and peaceful; savoring the moment, he was actually grateful for the forty-minute drive.

Steven was drifting off to sleep when the car pulled into the long wooded driveway. Realizing they were arriving, he sat up and tried to become alert. He felt fuzzy, just exhausted to his depths.

When the driver opened the door for him, he stepped out of the car and observed the amazing scenery. They were deep in the woods, surrounded by thick patches of trees. The house was a perfect combination of manageable size and classic style. It was an English Tudor, four bedrooms, three baths, Steven guessed. *Comfortable,* he thought. *Quaint.* This was a side of Vegas he'd never seen.

Steven felt the driver grab his forearm firmly. "Are you okay, Sir?" the driver asked.

"Yes, yes. I'm fine." Steven realized he was having a little trouble keeping his balance. "I guess I'm just really tired," he said with a nervous laugh. "It's been a tough few months, and I've been working very long days the last few weeks trying to catch up." He continued. "I lost my mother recently, and my daughter took some time off school to be with me. I just couldn't get back into the day-to-day." Steven was rambling. He never rambled. "What is wrong with me?" He asked himself aloud.

"Let's get you inside," the driver answered. As his already firm grip tightened on Steven's arm he led him up the walkway to the front door. Once inside he sat Steven in a club chair and put his feet up on an ottoman. "Are you comfortable?" the driver asked.

"Yes, thank you," he answered as he took the bottled water the driver was handing him.

"You may be dehydrated," the driver suggested, coaxing him to take another drink. "Your forehead is a little clammy."

"I don't understand what's wrong with me." Steven tried to get up, but his body felt so heavy, as if it was weighted down. He could barely move.

"Don't try to move." The driver gently pushed him back into a comfortable reclined position. "Just watch and enjoy the performance."

"What perform..." Steven's words were heavy and slurred.

"My name is Luke McCain, but you know me as Luke Boyd." The driver stood in front of Steven's chair and with slow, methodical movements, he took off his wig, revealing his dirty blond hair. He then began to peel off the face-forming mask he was wearing. "The thing about Vegas is, everybody's a performer." He laughed. "Even a make-up layman like me can actually make it look pretty good." He bent his head forward and removed the brown contacts he was wearing. When he looked up at Steven, their matching husky blue eyes met.

"Who are you?" Steven's heart was racing; his body was covered in sweat. He couldn't believe what he was seeing. It was like looking into a mirror. Steven shook his head, trying desperately to clear the fog.

Luke reached down and pulled the ottoman from under Steven's feet. He sat on it, directly facing Steven. "No, Steven. The real question is, who are you?" His tone was soft and almost comforting. "You were born Steven McCain." He let that sink in for a second. "A twin," he continued. "It seems our mother, a jobless alcoholic and borderline homeless person, desperate for money, decided to sell her unborn child. After all, she couldn't take care of herself, let alone a baby. I'll bet you can guess who the buyer was." He paused and met Steven's blank stare. "Stay with me bro." His voice took on a hint of sarcasm. "Mrs. Edward Montgomery. Only there was a problem. Adele Pruitt Montgomery was a proud woman who kept up appearances at all costs. She wouldn't consider telling any of her socialite friends she was barren. No, no, that wouldn't do. Instead, she faked her pregnancy. Now, here lies the problem, mom births twins! Adele, with all her money, could have easily afforded both of us. But it was so much more important to her to keep up appearances. And because of her selfishness, I grew up on the streets!" He spat out the last sentence. "I bounced from foster home to foster home! I could have grown up in a mansion! I could have attended the best schools! You!" He was yelling at Steven now. "You, being the first born by thirty-eight seconds!" He kicked the ottoman out of his way as he paced the floor.

"She was a good woman." Steven's voice was weak and he could barely form the words. "She was... not my mother?" Steven was trying to wrap his head around this information. He flashed back on his mother's dark hair, dark eyes and always tanned skin. He had never really let that sink in before. His father had dark hair too, but light eyes, he tried to justify his own fair features, but he couldn't, his own face was staring at him from across the room, and he couldn't deny that.

"How do you know this? How did you find me?" Steven mumbled, trying to clear his head and sort through the questions that were reeling around in his mind.

"Madison, my daughter," Luke paused, watching Steven slowly make the connection. "Yes." He smiled triumphantly. "That's right, Madison McCain is my daughter. That makes her your blood niece."

"Oh, God." Steven groaned. "I feel sick."

"Madison," Luke continued not missing a beat, "saw a picture of you and your late wife Kate in the paper when Kate passed away with cancer."

Steven smiled at the memory of Kate. "She was so beautiful. I was so proud of her," he reminisced.

"When Madi showed me the paper," Luke continued, interrupting Steven's memories. "I was completely shocked, too. We both started digging for the truth. Adele did a great job of covering her tracks, but in the end, my late mother's best friend finally confessed the whole story to us. Poor old girl, she died the next day in a kitchen fire." Luke let out a deep breath, mocking his sentiment. "Very sad."

"Why didn't you contact me right away?" Steven asked. "Reunite with me?"

"I started to, but then it hit me." Luke sat down on the ottoman in front of Steven again. He leaned in close and looked him directly in the eyes, husky blue staring at husky blue. "I could contact you and risk being rejected by you, you know, for the sake of appearances, like I was rejected by your mother, or I could just become you."

"I don't understand." Steven hated this fog his brain was in. Why couldn't he clear it? He shook his head again.

"Don't fight it, Steven. It's poison. You'll be dead within the hour." Luke's tone showed no emotion. "You see, I'm going to be you. I'm going to assume the role of Steven Montgomery, real estate mogul...entrepreneur...philanthropist." He was talking slowly as if trying to make a child understand. "Oh, I've been planning it for over a year. I killed Adele," he confessed. "She would have spotted an imposter in a second. She looked at me just before she died, I mean really looked at me; she knew who I was. I could see the regret in her eyes for the decision she made so long ago. And I'm sure you've figured out that Samantha must die as well."

"No!" Steven tried to scream, but he couldn't. "Oh God, no." Tears ran down his cheeks.

"Madison, my daughter, uh, I mean my wife," he emphasized the word wife to make sure Steven fully understood his intentions, "will guide me through becoming you. She'll vouch for me. Convince the world that I'm the real deal." He was laughing now. "It's a great plan! And you, my dear brother, helped us pull it off!"

"You're not well," Steven whispered, desperately trying to move his arms or legs, but they felt like they weighed a ton, and he just couldn't lift them. He couldn't fight this. "You're sick." He was struggling to keep his eyes open. They were so heavy. His whole body felt numb. *I'll just close my eyes for a second and rest,* he thought. Steven Montgomery never opened his eyes again.

CHAPTER 27

Officer Grayson Ryan sat in his black 1998 Honda CR-V. The rims had once been chrome. The car was scoured with scratches and parking lot battle wounds. It really wasn't much to look at. There were a million just like it on the road. And for that reason, it blended well and made for a good surveillance vehicle. He sipped his coffee and let his thoughts wander as he kept his eyes focused on the front door of the bookstore. *What a way to spend your day off,* he grumbled to himself. *You could have kept an eye on her by asking to spend the day with her,* he continued. *But everyday? Every waking, off-duty hour?* He laughed to himself. *Gray, it's official; you're a stalker.* He sat there debating how weird would it seem if he bumped into her in the store, where it was nice and warm. He opened the car door, then closed it again. He leaned his head back against the headrest, his frustration mounting.

When the door of the store opened and he saw her stepping out, he regained his focus. She looked amazing to him. Long hair blowing gently, showing off that beautiful broad smile, *I love her smile.* He thought. She was tugging on her black leather gloves and tightening the cobalt blue scarf around her neck. It was a cold, wintery day, rare for the south. He watched her walk over to the Mercedes she had borrowed from her step-mother and place her shopping bag in the trunk. She hopped into the driver's seat and pulled out of the parking space. He continued to watch as she made her way out of the parking lot. She turned left at the light and veered to the right onto the freeway entrance. It appeared she was heading home. As he predicted, she took the exit three miles up. Now that he was sure she was headed home, he could stay back far out of sight. Once she was home safe, he'd go grab a bite and maybe give her a call to see if she had any evening plans. Maybe he could buy her dinner again. As he steered his old, faithful Honda through the winding mountains, he was enjoying the music and tapping his steering wheel to the beat. He was excited about the prospect of having dinner with Samantha again tonight. His four-cylinder Honda was grumbling as he reached the height of the mountain. "I know girl," he told the old car. "Hang in there with me; we're about to start coasting down the backside." He gave the Honda's steering wheel a reassuring pat. The backside of the mountain top gave him a clear view of the road several miles ahead. He could see the Mercedes. It was speeding through the mountain curves. "She's lucky I'm not on duty," he said playfully out loud. "She's got to be pushing seventy!" He tried to catch her but couldn't close the gap. "Who drives like that on this winding road?" He yelled to himself, worry and anger setting in. Then he realized what was happening. He yelled at the top of his lungs, but he didn't hear a sound. The world shifted to slow motion as he watched the Mercedes fly off the cliff, with the grace of a bird gently riding on the wind currents. It crashed into the bottom of the gorge and burst into flames.

It felt like an eternity before he reached the crash site. He slammed on the brakes and jumped out of his car. He ran to the edge of the mountain and dropped to his knees. He moaned in pain as he watched the ball of fire below. The car was completely engulfed in flames. He knew Samantha couldn't have survived, and the realization shattered his heart. He forced himself to his feet and dragged himself back to his car to retrieve his cell phone; he needed to call 9-1-1. When he reached his car the door was still open. He held onto it for support as his body bent over and sobs raked him.

"Gray." Her voice was so soft he almost missed it.

"Samantha!" he shouted, looking around wildly. He saw her cobalt scarf across the road. Then he saw Samantha, lying up against the mountain. Tears of relief streamed down his face as he ran up to her and scooped her into his arms. "You're bleeding," He observed. "Can you move at all? We need to get you to a hospital." He gently lifted her off the ground. "Tell me if I'm hurting you," he whispered. She looked so fragile.

Silent tears ran down her face, but she didn't say a word. She was in pain; everything hurt, but she was safe.

He put her in the back seat of his car. He could see that she was shivering and her pupils were dilated. *Shock,* he thought. He put his coat over her and jumped into the driver's seat. He drove as fast as he could to the hospital at the base of the mountain. He pulled directly in front of the emergency room's electric double doors. Gently, he helped Samantha out of the backseat. She seemed disoriented; she was trying to tell him something, but she wasn't making any sense. Her clothes were covered in blood, but he couldn't tell where it was coming from, so he moved her slowly, trying not to cause her more pain or injury. A nurse pushing a wheelchair seemed to appear out of nowhere, Grayson lowered Samantha into the chair and the nurse wheeled her away. Within seconds, Grayson watched her disappear through the double doors.

He parked his car and headed inside. She was already in the exam room, so he sat in silence in the waiting room, staring at his blood-smudged hands folded in his lap. He didn't know what to do next. He just waited, then prayed, then waited some more.

When the nurse stepped into the waiting area, she looked directly at Grayson. She was a heavy-set, black woman with a no-nonsense stare. "Mr. Ryan?" She said. Grayson jumped up. "Are you family?" She asked.

"Yes," he lied.

"Well, she's asking for you. I have to warn you, she's weak and needs to rest. Please don't try to entertain her; stay with her, she wants you there, but let her sleep."

"Yes ma'am," he replied.

She led the way to Samantha's room. When Grayson stepped through the door and saw her lying there, bruised and bandaged, his heart broke; tears filled his eyes, and his throat desperately tried to swallow past the lump that had formed there. He stood near the door in total silence while he fought to regain his composure.

When she opened her eyes and saw him standing there, she flashed him her broad smile. "Gray," she whispered and her smile faded with the pain.

"I'm here." He moved to a chair beside her bed. "Don't talk." He rubbed her hand gently. "Just rest. Okay? You need to rest."

They sat in silence. Within minutes she was asleep again.

Grayson sat back in the chair and propped his feet up on the window sill beside her bed. His mind was reeling with possibilities. He wondered why she would drive so fast on a winding mountain road in the first place. He wondered how on earth she was thrown from the car. *Was she not wearing her seatbelt?* He wondered. He had no way to get a hold of her father. Steven was out of town on business, and the only contact phone number the station had for him was his home. Grayson didn't call it. He didn't want to talk with Madison; she gave him a bad vibe. The rush of emotions and the drama of it all left him drained. It wasn't long before he too, fell asleep, with Samantha's hand tucked safely in his.

When the doctor walked into Samantha's room, a startled Grayson jumped to his feet. It took him a second to focus and realize where he was.

"I just want to check on her." The doctor motioned toward Samantha. "And give you an update before I leave for the day."

"Okay. Good. Thank you," a sleepy Grayson replied.

"She's got a minor concussion, some deep cuts, as you can see by the stitches, and some pretty nasty bruising, but no broken bones or internal bleeding; the scan came back clear. She's going to be very sore for the next few weeks, but she should recover nicely. She's a very lucky girl. We're going to keep her overnight for observation. We intend to release her in the morning." The doctor placed his hand on Grayson's shoulder. "Go home, son," he advised. "Get some rest. Your wife is sedated and will sleep easily through the night. We'll keep a close eye on her."

"Thank you," Grayson replied, with no intention of correcting the doctor's wrong assumption that Samantha was his wife. "I won't sleep at home with her here. I'd prefer to stay, if that's okay?"

"Well, that's fine. I would probably do the same," he answered smiling at Grayson. "I will see you once more in the morning before we release her. Good night."

"Thank you again," Grayson said as the doctor left the room.

Now that he was wide awake, Grayson realized he was starving. He really hadn't eaten anything all day. He decided now would be a good time to run to the hospital cafeteria before it closed. He leaned over Samantha and listened to her breathing one more time. Sure she was sleeping soundly, he hurried down to the cafeteria and ordered a burger to go. While he waited for his order, he watched the television hanging on the wall in the cafeteria's seating area. The news reporter was standing on the edge of a mountain cliff. Smoke billowed up from the cliff behind her. With fire trucks and police cars on either side of her, she was reporting on Samantha's car accident. Grayson moved closer to the television to hear it better.

"The police have confirmed it was a single vehicle accident," she reported. "They do not know, at this time, how many people were in the car." She paused and looked down at her notes. Looking up again she continued. "Again, they believe the car was a late model Mercedes, but we do not have confirmation on that yet."

"Your hamburger is ready," the cafeteria clerk called out to Grayson.

"Thank you," he said as she handed him the bag. He took it and headed back to Samantha's room.

CHAPTER 28

Home sweet home, Madison thought with disapproval, as she walked through the busy, loud Las Vegas terminal. She had no intention of staying any longer than she absolutely had to. She loved the new life she'd created for herself in South Carolina, and she was anxious to get back to it. She claimed her bag and headed for the roof-top of the parking garage where her father had parked her car. It took her over a half hour and numerous attempts at making the car's horn beep to find it.

After killing another hour in the heavy Las Vegas traffic, she finally pulled into the driveway of her childhood home. She noticed the sign above the mailbox. Written, in Old English lettering was, the name "Boyd". She knew her father did that to make her laugh, and it worked. She loved his warped sense of humor.

When she reached the end of the driveway, she was thrilled to see her father, Luke, standing on the front steps waiting for her. He missed her, she reasoned. And she missed him so much. She was daddy's girl, and she'd been away from him for too long.

She jumped out of the car and hurried up the steps and into his arms. He kissed the top of her head and squeezed her in his arms tighter. "Oh, my baby girl," he professed. "I thought this day would never get here." He kissed the top of her head again. "I'm so proud of you, Madi." he continued. "I know how much you had to sacrifice, and now it's time for us to claim our reward."

"We better move quickly; the timing has to match up," she said, finally releasing him from her tight embrace. "Oh, and I love the 'Boyd' sign, but you should probably get rid of it before the cops come," she pointed out.

"Already on it," he said, showing her the screwdriver in his hand. "Body's in the family room. He's wearing my prescription reading glasses." He smiled. "Nice touch, huh?"

"Very nice," she agreed and headed inside. Steven's body was leaning back in her father's favorite chair, his feet propped up comfortably on the ottoman, his head slightly bowed as if he'd fallen asleep. Her father's glasses perched at the end of his nose. She noticed a book that appeared to have fallen from his grip and landed on the floor beside his chair. *Nice job, Daddy,* she thought. It looked completely natural, and more importantly, believable. She picked up the suicide note and read it aloud.

FACE FRONT

Dear Madison,

I hope you can find it in your heart to forgive me. I don't know what came over me. Even though I have promised you over and over again, for many years, that I would stop my out-of-control gambling, I'm afraid I am really in too deep this time. I have gambled and lost everything I own. I have mortgaged my house and my business and there is just no way for me to recover. I'm better off dead; you're better off with me dead. I'm so sorry, my sweet, that daddy has failed you.

Madison's eyes welled up with tears as she set the note back down and turned to face her father.

"Oh, you're good," her father applauded. "You missed your calling; you should be in Hollywood," he continued. "Okay, I've got all evidence of mine and Steven's potential business partnership, all the Montgomery family research we did, and my driver costume in the limo. Give me about twenty minutes to put some distance between me and this house, and then call the police." He glanced around to ensure he wasn't forgetting anything. "I will get rid of everything, return the car, and catch a cab to the hotel. Pick me up there in two days, and we're out of here. Oh, and by the way,

I recorded a news broadcast I thought you may be interested in; it seems a car went off a cliff and burst into flames. I believe it contained one Samantha Montgomery."

She leaned into him and wrapped her arms around him tightly one more time before he left. "Okay, daddy I know what to do."

Madison double-checked the house to make sure everything was in order. It looked good. Her father was thorough. She picked up the suicide note and read it again. She tried to get into her role as the shocked and grieving daughter. She tried to imagine how it would feel to really walk in to find her father dead and to read this note. She looked at her watch. *Another five minutes,* she thought. She read the note again. The tears began to really fall now. She read it again. She'd give the local cops an Oscar-worthy performance. She picked up the phone and dialed 9-1-1.

CHAPTER 29

Schwinn was standing in the dining room of his home adding pictures and post-it notes to the timeline of his biggest case, the murder of Adele Pruitt Montgomery. It had been quiet lately, and that wasn't good. Things were cooling off, and that's what made cases cold. The television in the living room was reporting the local breaking news: a car drove off a cliff and burst into flames. It didn't really catch Schwinn's attention; that sort of thing happened from time to time. The cliffs are dangerous and people are careless.

When the front door opened, he looked over to see Miranda, looking like a pack mule, carrying way too many grocery bags for one trip. She gave the door a little kick with her foot to make it swing wide. "Okay, I may need a little help," she admitted.

"Sweetheart." He rushed to her side and started taking the bags from her.

"It didn't seem like that much," she said, laughing.

"Who's moving in?" he asked sarcastically.

She gave him a sideways glance. "This is all you! I'm on a diet."

"You're always on a diet; and you're skinny; go figure."

"That's why I'm skinny!" she protested. "Hon, could you turn that down? I could hear it all the way down the drive." She gestured toward the television.

He reached for the remote and aimed it toward the television. He cocked his head sideways, just a bit, and narrowed his eyes as he examined the picture on the screen. It was a tire with a custom chrome rim. The reporter was explaining that it probably blew off the car in the explosion. It was the only clue to who owned the car. "It can't be," he said aloud, making no sense to Miranda.

"What?" she asked.

"So far, nobody has been reported missing, and we have not received any legitimate calls on this accident," the reporter continued. "The chrome rim most likely came from a local shop, and the police are trying to trace that now."

"That car belongs to Madison Montgomery," Schwinn explained to his wife. "I recognize the chrome rim from tailing her." He reached for his cell phone, but it rang in his hand before he could dial Roger's number.

"Rog," he answered. "Yes, I'm watching right now. Yes, I was just telling Miranda, it's hers. Okay, I'll meet you there."

"Sweetheart, let me help you," he said to Miranda as he picked the bags back up and headed for the kitchen. "I'm going to meet Rog at the police station in about an hour for an update. He's going to the Montgomery home right now."

"Do you think it was an accident?" Miranda asked, following him into the kitchen.

"Well." He paused, unsure how to answer. "Honestly, Madison was my main suspect. I couldn't pin it on her, but I felt strongly that it was her." He placed both hands on the counter and sighed heavily, a sign of frustration for him. "Does that make sense?"

She nodded yes. "If it's an accident, she may still have been your murderer."

"Could it have been Steven Montgomery all along?" He asked himself aloud.

"How will you know if it was really an accident?"

"It's going to take some time for Rog and his crew to investigate the scene, but most likely, he'll be able to tell." He started emptying bags. "Samantha?" he questioned, shaking his head. "This doesn't make sense."

"I'll put these away," she offered. "Go upstairs and change. Get out of here." She knew he was anxious to meet up with Roger and figure this thing out. She recognized that look of concentration on her husband's face.

He hurried up the stairs. He wasn't much help to her right now anyway.

CHAPTER 30

Luke pulled up to the booth at the dumpsite. He looked out of place in the limo and it bothered him that the guy manning the cashier's booth was focusing on him so intensely. "I've got two boxes," he told the cashier. "No more than twenty pounds each."

"Two boxes, forty pounds total," the cashier confirmed. "That'll be thirty-two dollars."

"Thirty-two bucks," Luke mumbled under his breath. "I thought the casinos were a rip-off."

"I'm sorry, sir, I didn't hear you." The cashier grinned at him. It was a sarcastic grin. A grin that said, I heard every word you said.

"Nothing," a disgruntled Luke replied as he handed the cashier two twenty dollar bills.

"Eight's your change. Thank you and come again." The cashier was laying on the polite customer service routine real thick.

"No, thank you," Luke said trying to lay it on thicker. He paused to read the cashier's name patch. "Chip," He said, his voice changing from sarcasm to surprise. He looked at the cashier, who was at least six feet tall, and probably two hundred and fifty pounds. Chip wore dirty garbage dump coveralls that looked as grungy as he did. "Seriously?" he questioned. "Chip?"

Chip laughed at Luke. "It's a nickname," he explained all the sarcasm gone from his voice.

Luke shook his head as he drove off. When he got to the edge of the dump-site, he popped his trunk and opened the boxes to verify their contents. His driver's costume, two disposable cell phones, his computer, smashed into a hundred pieces, and a box full of shredded documents, his research that revealed he was a twin and that his birth brother was adopted by Adele Montgomery. Anything that could reveal his true identity and his criminal actions. He tossed the boxes over the edge and watched them roll down the hill. He felt a sense of relief that it was almost over. As he drove out of the dumpsite, he passed the cashier's booth and gave Chip a nod.

"Something about that guy is creepy," Chip said to his co-worker, Bobby.

"Who dumps in a limo?" Bobby questioned.

"Good point. I'm going to go check out what he tossed."

"Might be worth something!" Bobby realized. "Okay, I'll cover the booth, but we split the find."

"Deal."

Luke reached for Steven's cell phone and dialed Madison. "Hi, Daddy," she answered.

"Baby, you've got to start calling me Steven," he reminded her.

"Sorry."

"I'm leaving the dumpsite now. I'm heading to return the limo. I was going to have the rental place give me a ride to the hotel, but since that journey is where I go from Luke McCain to Steven Montgomery, I think it's safer to call a cab, maybe even make some random stops along the way and switch cab companies."

"I agree."

"I should be settled in the hotel in an hour or so. I'll hole up there until you pick me up in a couple days."

"I'm on my way to the morgue. As soon as they rule it a suicide and release the body, I'll arrange for it to be sent to the funeral home and cremated. I'll have the urn placed with grandma's headstone. Everything is going exactly as planned."

"Good."

"You thought of everything, Da... Steven," she corrected herself.

"That's my girl." His voice was warm and praising. "I'll see you in two days. I love you, Madi."

"I love you, too."

CHAPTER 31

Samantha sat in the passenger seat of Grayson's Honda. "Are you sure about this?" She asked. The stitches on the side of her mouth made it difficult and a little painful to talk.

"Positive," he replied. "Sam, I know this sounds crazy; I almost don't want to say it in my out loud voice. But, I feel like you're in danger. I can't explain it. I just feel like I need to protect you. I've been feeling it for about a month." He glanced over at her. She was bruised and bandaged, yet she still looked so beautiful to him. "I have a confession. I was actually following you yesterday. I saw the accident." He was afraid to look her way. "I couldn't sleep the night before. I just had this weird feeling. Maybe a premonition; I don't even know if I believe in premonitions." He stared straight ahead, afraid to look at her, but he could feel her stare burning into him. "I needed to make sure you were safe. I'm not a crazy stalker," he promised. "I know I sound crazy right now."

She reached over and touched his arm. "I have a confession," she interrupted him. "I don't think my accident was an accident.

I tried to tell you in the hospital, but I was having trouble with my words."

"The meds," he stated. "They had you on heavy duty pain meds," he explained, seeing the confused look on her face.

She nodded her head in agreement. "I was trying to slow down; my brakes wouldn't work; I was pressing down on the pedal as hard as I could. I thought if I jumped, I would die, but if I didn't jump I would die." She shook her head. She wasn't saying it right. She knew she wasn't making any sense. "I jumped," she concluded with a shrug of her shoulders. "I wanted to tell you, but I couldn't. Then when I was lying there thinking about it..." She hesitated, not knowing how to say the next part. "I wondered how, or I guess why, you were there." She lowered her head. "I'm sorry, Gray. I guess I thought for a minute..." She didn't finish the thought.

"Sam," he said, folding her fingers in his. "I understand."

"There's more," she continued. "My friend, Megan, died in my dorm room. She was electrocuted. I watched her die!" Tears began to roll down her face. "They said it was faulty wiring. But I don't think so. And now this, I don't believe in coincidence."

"I don't either, and you're right to suspect something is up. I don't know what, or why, but I'm seriously worried about you." He glanced over at her. "I'm asking you to trust me, if you can." He smiled at her. "My parents are great people: humble, loving people. They will take good care of you. I'm just asking you to hide out for a couple days while I try to figure this thing out. That's reasonable, right?"

"Yes," she agreed, wiping at her tears. "But you can call my dad and tell him the truth. It's killing me to think about him suffering right now, thinking I died in that crash."

"What about Madison?"

"I don't trust her."

"Neither do I. Are you sure your dad won't blurt out you're alive and well, hidden out at Camp Ryan?"

"Wait." She sounded surprised. "It's a camp?" She flashed him that beautiful smile and then winced from the pain it caused.

Grayson laughed at her silliness. "I'm glad you're back." He returned her smile. "And yes, we can call your dad. You'll just have to ask him to respect your wishes and not tell anyone, including Madison, for now."

Less than fifteen minutes later, he turned the car into the driveway of a gray, tri-level home, with black shutters completing each window, and a faux brick front wall. "I'm nervous," Samantha confessed.

"Why?"

"Because I'm meeting your parents, silly. And, I don't have the luxury of a pleasant hello, maybe a meal, and then a thank you and good night. No, I get to say, hi, I'm Samantha, and I'm dating your son and moving in for a couple days. So nice to meet you."

He turned off the engine and shifted his body to face her. Taking both her hands in his, he tried to reassure her. "Sammie," he began softly. "My parents, Gary and Betty, already know what's going on. You don't have to try to explain; they get it. They're fun loving people, and you're going to enjoy your time here with them. I promise," he concluded.

"I know," she conceded. She leaned forward and rested her forehead against his. He kissed her, gently, careful not to hurt the stitches and the bruise that crossed her cheek and lips. Then he got out of the car and walked around to the passenger side and opened her car door for her.

CHAPTER 32

Madison waited outside the hospital morgue with the police officer. *What was taking them so long?* she wondered. It was a dreary place, sterile and colorless. She kept her head down, trying to look like the wounded daughter of a man who just committed suicide.

"It shouldn't be too much longer." The Las Vegas police officer tried to console her.

She didn't reply. She just sat in the hard, plastic chair, and stared at her feet. She loved how skinny her ankles looked. She loved the color of polish she picked out for her pedicure. But most of all, she loved her new sandals. *Three hundred and forty bucks!* she thought. *For two little straps of leather.*

"Miss McCain?" the hospital coroner asked.

"Yes." Madison stood up

"We're ready for you." He held the door open for Madison as she followed him into the exam room.

Madison saw Steven's body, stiff and discolored, and a flood of tears she wasn't expecting ran down her cheeks. "That's my father," she whispered, finding it difficult to speak. "Luke McCain."

"I'm ruling it a suicide," the coroner told her. "I'm sorry for your loss."

She turned and hurried out of the morgue. She stepped into the closest restroom she could find. *What's wrong with me?* she thought. *Is it because he looks so much like my father?* She was trying to reason with herself. *Is it the relief of knowing it's ruled a suicide?* Then she realized with a sad regret, that she had spent over a year with Steven, and she'd grown to love him even though that wasn't part of the plan. She was feeling the heaviness of losing him. She dabbed at her tears with a tissue and checked herself in the mirror. She walked back into the morgue. The two police officers and the coroner were still standing there, hovering over Steven's body. They had pulled the sheet back over him. "What happens next?" she asked fighting to maintain her composure.

"You'll need to contact a funeral home to make arrangements," the coroner answered, his voice heavy with sympathy for her. This was the worst kind of death: an unnecessary one.

She nodded in agreement. The tears just kept coming. *Why can't I get a grip?* she thought. "Am I finished here?" she asked, still struggling to find her voice.

FACE FRONT

"Yes," the coroner confirmed and walked her to the door. "Miss McCain, will you be okay to drive home? Would you like me to call a taxi for you?"

"No. I'm good. Thank you." She shook his hand and walked out.

CHAPTER 33

Grayson opened the front door and ushered Samantha in. "Anybody home?" he called out. Betty came rushing up the stairs, full of excitement to meet her son's new girl. Her smile faded when she saw Samantha. Bruises covered every visible part of her body. She had stitches on her face and head. A portion of her hair shaved. Betty could see through it all the beauty Samantha once was.

"I was in my office, paying bills," she explained for no reason. She was desperately trying to hide the shock of seeing Samantha's condition.

The sound of the sliding glass door was a welcome distraction. Gary walked through carrying freshly picked tomatoes, deep red in color and the size of his palm. "Look at these beauties!" he said to Betty as he kicked off his muddy shoes. Leo, their miniature Pomeranian, ran around Gary's feet, full of energy.

"Gary, come meet Samantha."

He walked into the living room. He gave Samantha a glance and much to Betty's horror, he asked, "Good Lord, girl, what happened to you? Bar fight?"

Samantha tried to laugh, but it hurt. "Nice to meet you, too," she replied sarcastically. Immediately she liked Grayson's parents. They were exactly what he said they'd be.

Leo hiked up his upper body and begged to be petted. "He's so cute; a little ball of fur." Samantha bent down to pet him.

"He's a pest," Betty warned Samantha. "Once you show him a little attention, he won't leave you alone." She motioned for the dog to sit. "We're going to settle her in your old room," Betty said to Grayson. "C'mon, Samantha, Gray's room is right down here." She led the way downstairs. Grayson's room had a full-sized bed pushed up against the window. There was a bench with a throw blanket at the foot of it. He had two men's armoires standing side by side, each one with double door cabinets and three drawers. Betty opened the doors on one armoire and showed Samantha how to work the television and DVD player. "The other one is empty, so you can put your clothes in it."

Samantha looked down at the very baggy navy blue sweat pants and Red Sox sweat shirt she was wearing. "These belong to Gray," she said. "I don't have any clothes. They cut them off of me in the hospital." She lifted her foot in the air just a little to show off her new sneakers. "Gray bought me these!" She said with excitement. "Socks and underwear, too," she continued. "Cotton granny panties," she said with an embarrassed laugh in her voice.

"Well, dear, maybe Gray thought this wasn't the appropriate time for Victoria's Secret." They both laughed. Samantha pressed her hand against the stitches that covered the side of her mouth and cheek, in an effort to keep them from pulling.

"Maybe not," she agreed. She liked Betty; she was comfortable with her.

"Okay, this is your bathroom." Betty waved her hand in the direction of the bathroom. "On the counter you'll find some toiletries Gray picked up for you. The basics. Toothbrush, toothpaste, deodorant, hair brush," she counted them off on her fingers as she spoke. "If there is anything else you need, just let me know, and we'll send Gary to the store."

Thank you." Samantha felt so grateful. "I really appreciate your doing this for me. Gray tells me it will just be for a couple days. I'll try not to be a bother."

"You're welcome, hon, and you are not a bother. We're happy to have you here. It gives us a chance to get to know you a little." Betty reached out and touched Samantha's arm; she regretted it instantly when she saw Samantha wince. "Oh, I'm sorry."

"Don't worry. I'm just a little tender." Sam smiled at her trying to act like she wasn't in pain.

"Mom, what time is dinner?" Grayson called out from the living room. "I need to run an errand. Do I have time?"

"Maybe a little more than an hour," she called back. "Be warned Samantha. Gray eats like every meal is the last supper."

"Would you mind if I just lay down for a bit? I'm a little tired."

"Of course you are; take a nap. I'll send Gray down to check on you when dinner is ready. Tri-tip, garlic mashed potatoes, and broccoli." She tried to entice Samantha's appetite. "I have a nightgown for you, hanging on the back of the door in your bathroom." She hesitated, then added with a laugh, "I'm afraid it's a granny style, too."

After Betty left the room, Samantha sat on the bench at the foot of Grayson's bed. The walls were covered with sports photos. A couple of them were even autographed. She stood up and walked closer to read what they said. "Go, Sox! Big Papi," she read aloud. It was a picture of a Red Sox baseball player. His body twisted in full swing like he had just hit a home run; the back of his jersey said Ortiz. She read the next one. "To Gray. Joe Montana." She pondered the picture. The simplicity of it reminded her of a Little League football card. Montana, in full Forty-Niners football gear, kneeling on one knee, holding his helmet under his arm. She glanced up to see that on top of one of the armoires was a football enclosed in a glass case. The signature read Joe Namath. "Wow," she whispered. She knew who that was. Broadway Joe. Her grandfather was a big fan she remembered.

"That one belonged to my dad." Grayson startled her. "Sorry. I didn't mean to scare you," he apologized. He walked over to the football. "My dad gave this to me when I graduated college." She could see the pride in his eyes as he looked at it.

"Is dinner ready so soon?" She sounded surprised; only five, maybe ten minutes had passed.

"No, not yet. I just thought I'd check on you to make sure you have everything you need. I'm going to run an errand. I'll be gone for about an hour."

"I'm good. Thank you, Gray, for everything you've done for me." She lowered her head, looking at the baggy sweats. "I've got a nice wardrobe," she pointed out, tugging at the oversized seat of the sweatpants. "I don't think I fully appreciated it until now."

He laughed at her silliness. Even wounded and bruised, she had a sense of humor. He loved that about her. "You may want to close the door behind me. Leo will try to come in here and cuddle with you."

"I wouldn't mind. He's so cute."

"Yes, but he's a kisser, and he won't let you rest."

She smiled at the thought of it. "Okay. Close the door behind you then." She pulled the blankets back and crawled under them. Her body felt heavy and tired.

He gently tucked the blankets around her. "I'll check on you in a couple hours, when dinner is ready." He bent down and kissed her forehead.

"Gray," she called after him as he walked toward the door. He stopped and turned to face her. "After dinner, can we call my dad? It kills me to think he's worrying about me."

He nodded his head yes. "Get some rest, beautiful. It will help you heal."

"Okay. And Gray, your parents are great, just like you said."

"I'm glad you think so too." He closed the door behind him.

CHAPTER 34

After the fourth person interrupted to say hello to Schwinn, he and Roger decided to go grab a bite, and some privacy, so they could compare notes.

"Shannon's, half an hour," Schwinn confirmed as he headed for the door of the police station.

"Schwinn!" Detective Delgado extended a hand for Schwinn to shake. "How's retirement?"

"It's good," he replied. "Really good."

"Hey, Schwinn!" came the voice up the walkway behind Delgado. It was Detective Brown. "How you doing, man?" Brown leaned in for a man hug and shoulder pat.

"I'm good. Good," he repeated. "Hey, Kleven," Schwinn fist bumped Detective Kleven as he walked by. He wished he had more time to spend with these guys. They were like family, and he missed them.

"It looks like you and Miranda are spending some serious time at the beach, or is that fake and bake?" Delgado asked, and they all laughed.

"No. No. Miranda bought an antique wicker patio ensemble, you know, with a serving buffet.

"Oh, a serving buffet." Kleven repeated, nudging Brown with his elbow.

"What's an ensemble?" Brown questioned.

"Anyway, she's pretty proud of it," Schwinn continued, ignoring their playful teasing. "So we have breakfast and coffee out there almost every morning; even though the weather has been too cold for it. I just drink more hot coffee." He laughed. "What you're seeing isn't sun, it's wind burn."

"Don't knock it, man, you've got a beautiful home. Miranda has real decorating talent. She should have gone professional. Unlike Delgado here." Brown gestured toward Delgado. "I grab coffee at his house on the way in, and I'm sitting on a folding chair drinking from a Styrofoam cup!" They all laughed.

"Listen, guys, I'm really pressed for time. I'd love to catch up, though; what do you think? Pizza and beer? Just the guys?" Schwinn asked.

"I'm in," Delgado replied.

"Me too," Kleven agreed.

FACE FRONT

"Sounds good, just say when." Brown patted Schwinn's shoulder. "Let's do it soon huh?" The guys obviously admired Schwinn and missed having him around. The feeling was mutual.

Schwinn glanced in Roger's direction, confirming he was on his way, as he walked out the door.

When he got to Shannon's, he sat in a booth and ordered a pitcher of Coke and a platter of chicken wings. "On the clock," he explained to the waitress. Roger was sliding into the booth across from him just as the waitress was setting their pitcher on the table.

"That was quick," he said to Roger.

"Yeah, I've got news," Roger replied, diving right into business. "One of my rookies, Grayson Ryan, called me. This is hush." He knew he didn't have to remind Schwinn to keep any information he gave him quiet, but he did anyway. Habit. "He was tailing the Montgomery girl. He watched her drive off the cliff."

"Samantha or Madison?" Schwinn's voice raised, drawing attention from a couple seated near them. It bugged him that they had been sitting on the Montgomery home since they discovered it was Madison's Mercedes that crashed, and nobody has been home all night or day. And to make it even worse, nobody has been reported missing. It's like the entire Montgomery three went missing. "Were they all in the car?" he wondered aloud.

"Samantha," Roger replied in almost a whisper, trying to bring the volume back down to a private level.

"Samantha's dead?" Schwinn was surprised how sad this news made him feel. "Was she alone in the car?"

"No, she's not dead and yes, she was alone. She jumped and survived. Can you believe it?" Now Roger was excited but still desperately trying to be quiet. "Ryan saw the whole thing go down. He drove her to the hospital. He's got her holed up at his folks' house. He thinks somebody tried to kill her."

"I think he's right." Schwinn leaned back in the booth, trying to absorb this news. "Rog, this case is crazy. I can't make it make sense." He sighed heavily; frustration was setting in. "Follow the money, right? Well, with Adele out of the way, Steven owns about ninety percent of the Montgomery fortune. I don't think he'd kill his own daughter for the additional ten percent. Madison would need to get rid of all three, Adele, Samantha, and Steven, in order to control the money. But seriously, does she think all three could die without us giving her the fine-tooth-comb treatment?" He shook his head at the nonsensical idea of it.

"I've seen people do dumber things than that," Roger offered, "and so have you." He paused. "Maybe she doesn't plan to kill Steven. Maybe this isn't just money, maybe it's jealousy. She wants the mom and daughter out of the way so she doesn't have to share hubby with them." Roger stopped talking when the waitress approached their table with the wings Schwinn ordered.

"Thank you."

"Can I get you anything else?" She asked.

"No, thank you." Schwinn's answer came quick and much sharper than he intended. He was anxious to get back to his private conversation with Roger. The waitress turned and headed back to the kitchen without saying another word.

"Makes sense," Roger continued. "Mom dies of old age, daughter has a car accident. Not unreasonable. She's almost twenty years younger than her husband; she out-lives him; nothing suspicious in that," he reasoned.

"So who knows she's alive?"

"Ryan, the doctor and nurses, his folks, you and me." He thought about this for a second. "Actually, that's a lot of people when you think about it. Maybe we should move her to a safer location."

"Where?"

"How about your house?" Roger was smiling at Schwinn as he bit into a chicken wing.

"I'm good with it, and I think Miranda will be, but let me run it by her just to be sure."

"Ask her quick. This thing is all over the news, and one of the hospital staff is likely to call in and report seeing her at the hospital. If that leaks and Madison finds out she failed, she may try again."

CHAPTER 35

Samantha was perfectly comfortable propped up in bed, watching a romantic-comedy and doing her best to be still, rest, and heal, per doctor's orders. She was a goal-oriented person, and being still was down right hard for her. But she had to admit, this felt fabulous. "I could get used to this," she mused with a smile that caused her stitches to pull. She reached up and pressed her hand against the side of her mouth; putting pressure on the stitches made them feel better.

"Come in," she said to the knock at her bedroom door.

"Hey." Grayson poked his head in. "How's the patient?"

Still holding her stitches in place, she gave him a half smile. "I'm great. Gray, thank you for all you're doing for me. I just can't imagine how I ca..."

"Shhh. It's nothing," he interrupted her. He held up shopping bags. "Mom went with me to try to add a woman's touch."

"Clothes," she observed. "Real clothes," she said as she pulled a pair of skinny jeans, two blouses, a pullover sweater, and a coat out of the bags. "You must have spent a fortune. I'll pay you back. I promise."

"It wasn't bad. Mom is great at finding sales and bargains," he assured her. "They're a gift," he added. "I insist."

Samantha reached up and wrapped her arms around Gray's neck. She hugged him tight for what felt like an eternity. Her eyes welled up with tears. "Gray," was all she could say. She had no idea how to express what she was feeling: gratitude, love.

"I know," he said as he kissed the side of her head and gently rocked her back and forth. "I'm in love with you, Sammie. Please let me take care of you, spoil you even, the best way I know how."

She pulled away from him just enough to face him. "I love you, too. Somewhere between the two hour phone dates, late at night, and a million text messages, I fell in love with you, too." She kissed him. Then, ignoring the pain it caused, she kissed him again.

"Knock, knock," Betty said, causing them both to jump, then laugh. "I didn't mean to interrupt, but dad said the tri-tip is about ready. "Are you hungry hon?" she asked Samantha.

"Actually I am," Samantha replied. "And Betty, thank you so much for the clothes."

Betty waved it off. "It was nothing," she said as she turned and headed back to the kitchen.

"Are you ready to head up?" Gray asked.

"Do I look bad?" she questioned. "Should I change?"

Gray gave her a slow look over from head to toe. "Turn around." He gestured a circular motion with his hand.

She gave him a friendly smack. "Let's eat."

"You're beautiful," he finally answered. "In baggy sweats and no make-up, you're the most beautiful thing I've ever laid eyes on." He meant it. "But don't tell Betty I said so," he added with a laugh. "She thinks she's cornered that market."

The four of them sat at an oversized, round, solid oak table that could easily seat eight. Gary had grilled the tri-tip on his old faithful Weber. It smelled delicious. Betty made her famous garlic mashed potatoes. She thickly sliced the tomato and broccoli Gary grew in his greenhouse and added some garlic, cracked pepper, basil, and a red wine vinegar and olive oil mixture to them. Samantha was truly enjoying herself. She listened to Gary and Betty tell stories of Grayson's childhood, most of them embarrassing, all of them funny. Grayson tried, without success, to change the subject. His childhood was very different from hers. She had great parents, loving parents, but her world was much more serious than his. She never realized that before. Her childhood was filled with ballet lessons, riding lessons, charity events, and social gatherings. She had a good childhood, a good life; she had no complaints. She had just never seen it from this angle before. Grayson reached over and placed his hand on hers. She flashed him that beautiful broad smile of hers, then immediately winced. He gave her hand a gentle squeeze and returned his focus to his dinner plate.

"Did you save room for dessert?" Betty asked Samantha. "Gary made me buy a cheesecake and strawberries."

"I thought Samantha might like something sweet after dinner," Gary added.

"Never mind that it's your favorite," Betty played with him.

"I'd love a piece," Samantha replied. "Thank you."

"Smart girl," Gary gestured toward Samantha.

Betty brought the cheesecake out and set it on the table. Beside it she placed a big bowl of strawberries and a can of whipped cream. "Don't be shy," She said as she placed dessert plates and forks on the table. "I'll get some napkins."

Grayson and Gary made an awkward serving pair, but between the two of them, they managed to put a piece of cheesecake, upright, on a plate. Gary topped it with a scoop of strawberries, and Grayson handed it to Samantha. Licking the thumb he used to push the cheesecake upright on her plate, he offered her the can of whipped cream. She laughed at his awkwardness and accepted the can. Betty brought out a fresh pot of coffee and placed it on a warmer on the table. The foursome enjoyed a fresh round of light-hearted conversation. Samantha felt like she'd known them forever. They were fun and easy to be around. She shared some childhood memories with them, told them about her mother passing, and shared her college and career plans. They seemed genuinely interested. When she spoke of her father, guilt struck her. She knew her father must be sick with grief, thinking he'd lost her.

"Gray, could we call my father?" she asked. "I understand your concerns, but we can ask him to keep my secret safe and not tell anyone, not even Madison. He'll respect my wishes, whether he agrees with us or not."

"Sam." Grayson wasn't sure what to do. "I don't want your dad to worry or grieve, but I feel like we need to be really cautious."

"It's my dad," she pressed. "He will keep our secret."

How could he say no to her? "Okay," he gave in. "But let me talk with him first. Let me explain everything before I reveal you're alive and in hiding. I don't want him to hear your voice and tell Madison it's you on the phone before we can tell him you're in hiding. Agreed?" he asked.

"Agreed." She turned her attention to Betty and Gary. "Thank you so much for dinner. It was delicious." She stood up, and as she headed toward her room she stopped and hugged Betty. "Thank you again for the clothes."

"You're welcome, hon. Let me know if you need anything else."

Grayson helped his mom clear the table. "You wash, I'll dry?" he asked.

"I've got this," Betty replied. "You go with Samantha, and call her father. Don't make that poor man worry another second."

"Thanks, mom." Grayson kissed Betty's cheek.

Back in his bedroom, Samantha and Grayson sat side by side on the bench at the end of his bed. Grayson dialed the number Samantha gave him. "It went straight to voicemail," he said as he pressed the speaker phone button so she could hear her father's voice instructing the caller to leave a message. "This is Officer Ryan, uh, Mr. Montgomery, its Grayson. Grayson Ryan," he spoke into the phone. "Could you please call me at 5-5-5-9-2-0-8?" He hung up. They sat in silence for a few minutes. Samantha leaned in and rested her head on Grayson's shoulder.

"Thank you for trying."

"You're welcome."

"Are you heading home soon?"

"Actually, yes, but I'm just going to pack an overnight bag, feed Bosley, and take him for a quick walk; I'll be back in an hour. I'm going to spend the night here tonight; I'll crash on the couch. I've got to get up early, though, to head home in the morning and check on Bosley once more before I go to work."

"So if my dad calls you back tonight, I'll get to talk with him?" Her voice sounded so hopeful.

"Exactly." He gently ran his hand down the side of her hair, catching a few strands between his thumb and forefinger. "Why don't you crawl under the covers and finish your movie? Come get me if you need anything."

She nodded in agreement. "In case I fall asleep, wake me if he calls."

"I promise."

"Grayson, who's Bosley?" she asked.

"He's my dog. I'll introduce you to him when you're feeling better."

"How come you don't just bring him back here with you tonight? You know, save yourself a trip home in the morning."

"Because Miss Betty would have my hide!" He laughed. "Besides, Bosley outweighs Leo by about sixty pounds, and I fear Leo would become a chew toy."

"Oh, we can't have that!"

"No, we can't." He stroked her hair once more. "Now get some rest." He leaned in and kissed her forehead before he left the room.

CHAPTER 36

The solid mahogany antique dining room table, with its white marble top could not be seen underneath all the files spread out on its surface. Schwinn and Roger sat across from each other, reading through newspaper clippings, birth records, marriage certificates, anything and everything they could get their hands on that referenced the Montgomery family and their fortune.

"I know we're missing something." Schwinn leaned back in his chair and rubbed his hands over his face, trying to relieve the weariness he felt. "I'm frustrated with this case." He paused for a moment and scratched the side of his head. "I'm exhausted." He sighed heavily. "And I'm frustrated," he reiterated.

"I know; me, too." Roger agreed. "But at least you're on the payroll. This isn't even an open case for me."

"C'mon, Rog, you know I'll kick you some money come payday."

"I didn't mean it like that." Roger stood up and paced the room. "I don't even know why I said it. I really didn't mean it like it came out."

Schwinn laughed. "I know, but you're my best friend, and you've been an invaluable resource for me. Of course I'm going to take

145

care of you." Schwinn leaned back in the chair, forcing it to rest on only its two back legs.

"If Miranda saw you do that, you'd be couch bound for a week." Roger said with a warning laugh.

"If Miranda saw what?" Came Miranda's voice from the kitchen.

Schwinn hurried to right the chair on all fours again. "Nothing doll." He shot Roger a sideways look. Roger knew that look. It was the look that said, I'm-gonna-get-you-later. "What are you doing up so late?" Schwinn asked Miranda as she entered the room.

"Isn't it obvious?" she asked. She was carrying a plate of cold cut sandwiches and a big bag of chips. "I thought you two might be hungry; you've been at it for hours again."

"Starved," Roger spoke up. "Thanks."

She set the tray on top of the files in the middle of the table. "Can I get you something to drink?" she asked. "Do you want me to make a pot of coffee?"

"No. I want you to get some rest. It's late." Schwinn gave her a pat. "Thank you. I don't think I realized how hungry I am."

"How about a couple of Coke's?" she pressed. "That's easy. Then I'll go right back to bed. I promise." She smiled at her husband.

"Coke would be great. Thanks," Roger answered with his mouth full of turkey and swiss on multi-grain bread, with tomato, avocado, and mayo. "Mmmm. This is good. I really was starving."

"Thank you, doll." Schwinn rubbed the small of Miranda's back. It was these small things, things like getting out of bed at eleven o'clock at night to make him a sandwich, that he really appreciated about his beautiful wife. *That's love,* he thought as he watched Miranda walk out of the room.

"You know, Rog, I've never seen Madison and Steven show affection." Schwinn paused and focused on his friend who was almost done with his sandwich.

"Well, two things come to mind. One, Madison married Steven for the money; we all know that. And two, old money swells rarely show affection publicly; it wouldn't suit their image."

Schwinn pondered this for a moment. "You're probably right," he agreed and dropped the subject. He reached for a sandwich and took a bite. He glanced at a piece of paper that he had scribbled some bullet points on. "So, Steven went to Vegas for a business meeting, and Madison went the next day to surprise him."

"Mmm-hmm." Roger confirmed, nodding his head yes.

Miranda walked back into the dining room and set two cold Cokes on the table. She gave her husband a kiss on his head.

"Good night, boys," she said as she walked back out of the room and headed up the stairs.

"Nobody reported Samantha missing, well, because they were in Vegas and had no idea she was missing," Schwinn pointed out. "And Grayson confirmed this with Samantha?"

"That's right."

Glancing back at his notes, he continued. "Their flight home arrives tomorrow evening at nineteen-fifteen?" Not waiting for an answer, he looked back at his long-time friend. "I say we meet them at the airport and see how they take the news."

"Let's tail them from the airport. Deliver the news to them at home. They may be reserved at the airport and justify it because of the crowd. At home we should see their real reaction."

"You're right," Schwinn agreed. "Wanna call it a night? Grab some dinner tomorrow night and drive to the airport together?"

"Good plan. Call me tomorrow with a time and place."

Both men stood, stretched, and headed for the front door. "Thanks, Rog." Schwinn patted Roger's shoulder. "I do appreciate all your help, and I will pay you for the time you've put in with me."

"I know." Roger gave him a return pat on the shoulder and headed out the door.

Schwinn went back into the dining room. He picked up the empty plates and Coke cans, and scanned the room for anything else he needed to put away before heading to bed. A paper on the top of one of the open files caught his eye. He tried to focus, but his eyes were tired and blurry. "State of South Carolina," he read aloud. It looked like a birth certificate but not quite a birth certificate. He squinted his eyes in an effort to focus, but it just wasn't working. "Tomorrow is another day," he told himself, giving up with a yawn. He clicked off the dining room light with his elbow and headed to the kitchen to put the dishes in the sink. He was exhausted and just couldn't bring himself to think about the Montgomery Three anymore tonight.

CHAPTER 37

The plane touched down so hard that it actually lifted off the ground and touched down again. The flight attendant made light of it by joking about the passengers getting double reward miles. Madison wasn't interested in jokes. She was trying to make sure her father, Luke McCain, was ready to face South Carolina, and the world, as Steven Montgomery. "Now, remember, Dad, if you…"

"Steven," he cut her off. "for the last time, Steven."

"Steven." She shook her head as if trying to clear it. "Why can't I get that?" She sounded exasperated.

Luke reached over and rubbed her knee. "Don't worry, baby. You'll be fine." He ran his hands through his hair again. "I can't get used to this cut."

"You look great," she reassured him. "The hi-lights are perfect; you look just like Steven."

He gave her knee a squeeze and stood up to exit the airplane. Once inside the terminal, Madison wrapped her arm inside her father's as they made their way to the front curb of the airport. She felt tired to her core. The stress of this past year had taken its toll on her. But, it was almost over. *Report Samantha missing, confirm another body, and get through the funeral and it's happily ever after for Steven and Madison Montgomery,* she thought. But, there was that one little thing that didn't sit well in her soul. She could never really fall in love and marry. After all, she was already married. She leaned in closer to her father as they walked. *We're worth millions now,* she thought. *That's worth giving up love and marriage. Besides, Daddy always says love is overrated.* She tried to reason with herself. It wasn't working. She thought about Samantha and Grayson. She'd seen them together, interacting. *They were in love,* she thought. Sad, she actually felt a tinge of guilt.

"Well, well. It seems Vegas was good for the newlyweds," Schwinn broke the forty minute silence he and Roger had been savoring. "Look how cozy they are now."

"Ironic. We were just talking about their lack of affection," Roger observed. "Why the sudden change?"

"No clue," Schwinn answered. "Jewelry?" he jokingly added as he started the car and pulled away from the curb. He kept a good distance behind the limo that carried Luke and Madison to the Montgomery mansion less than twenty minutes from the airport.

FACE FRONT

There wasn't much traffic and it was easy to spot the overdone, stretch limo in the distance.

"Officer Ryan, Grayson Ryan, left a message," Luke told Madison, interrupting her peaceful trance.

"What did he want?"

"He didn't say. He only left a number. Shall we find out?" He began to dial Grayson's number. Madison reached over and placed her hand over his phone.

"Let's not; I'm not up for Grayson; he's Samantha's boyfriend," she explained. "He probably wants to come over and deliver the bad news. I'm sure Sam talked with him before her accident. She probably told him we were in Vegas. He doesn't know we're back yet. Let's call him later. Or tomorrow even."

"Sweetheart, I know who Grayson Ryan is. You taught me well." He smiled at his daughter. "When we get home, you get some rest, and I'll peruse the mansion and get familiar with it. Tomorrow we'll call Grayson back and let the world know we're home. But tonight, we'll enjoy a little peace and privacy. Deal?"

"Deal." She smiled at him, pleased with this plan.

Less than two miles from the Montgomery mansion, Schwinn pulled over. "What's the plan?" he asked Roger.

153

"We could give them a couple minutes to get inside and go break the news to them about Samantha's accident. See their reaction."

"If we tell them about the accident, we have to tell them she's alive," Schwinn reasoned. "I'm not sure I want to give Madison that information."

"I agree. Samantha won't be safe once Madison finds out she's alive." Roger tilted his head and cracked his neck. "Any ideas?"

"Actually, I do have an idea." He paused, trying to put it all together in his head. He reached for his blue tooth earpiece and placed it in his ear. Then he dialed Roger's number. "Answer it," he instructed as Roger looked at him, confused.

"Hello?" Roger said into his cell phone feeling silly answering Schwinn's call, while he was sitting right next to him in the car.

"Here's what we'll do." Schwinn spoke into his blue tooth. "I'll drop you off just up the road, out of sight of the mansion. I'll go to the door alone. I'll tell them I had an appointment with Samantha. Steven won't question that, and Madison can't because Samantha isn't there to contradict it. Of course, they'll tell me Samantha isn't home. I'll strike up a conversation with Steven. I'm a private, so I'm not obligated to tell them anything about Samantha's accident or survival. Hopefully, later, when Steven finds out I knew, Madison will be behind bars, and Steven will understand why I kept silent."

"What are you going to say?"

"I don't know. I want to bait Madison, but I have no idea what to say. It'll come to me," he reasoned. "I just want to listen for the classic, past tense talk about Samantha. That'll tell us if she already knows or not. And you'll hear the whole thing." He tapped his earpiece.

"That's good," Roger confirmed. "Let's go."

Schwinn drove as close to the mansion as he could without being seen, then he pulled to the curb again. "I won't be inside long. If you need to speak to me, speak low. I don't want to risk them hearing you."

"Copy." Roger jumped out of the car and watched Schwinn pull away. Within minutes he could hear Schwinn telling him he was approaching the front door. Moments later he heard Madison answering the door.

"Hello, Madison. How are you?" Schwinn put on a warm smile and extended his hand for Madison to shake. She did, reluctantly. "I have an appointment with Samantha." He got straight to business.

"She's not here," Madison reported happily. "I'll have her call you to reschedule." She started to close the door.

"Could I have a moment with Steven then?" Schwinn put his hand out to stop the door from closing in his face. *This broad is a piece of work,* he thought. *What does Steven see in her?*

"Steven's, uh…"

"I have news about his mother's murder," he added quickly, putting emphasis on the word murder, trying to spark her interest.

"Murder?" she asked. "The police said she died of natural causes."

"Well, that was the official report at the time of her death, but as you know, Steven suspected murder, and I agree. So I've been digging into her life and murder ever since he hired me." He could see the surprise on Madison's face. He paused to let his words sink in. "I believe the police will be reopening her case." Was it his imagination? Or did all the color just drain from Madison's face? *This is our murderer,* Schwinn thought. *We've just got to prove it.*

"Please, come in." Madison opened the door wide. "Have a seat in here." She pointed to the formal living room, they rarely used. "I'll get Steven." She was gone for what seemed like an eternity. Then she reappeared with Steven by her side. Again she had her arm wrapped in his.

A united front, Schwinn observed. *Are they in this together?* He didn't want to believe that. He really liked Steven, and he wanted to believe he was innocent.

"Good evening, Mr. Schwinn." Luke extended his hand for Schwinn to shake.

So formal. What's up with that? Schwinn thought, shaking his hand.

"Madison tells me you've come to deliver news about my late mother."

"Yes. Well, actually I came here to see Samantha. We had an appointment. Do you know when she'll return?"

"No, I don't. We just got home ourselves. What news do you have of my mother's case?" He was anxious to hear what evidence might have been uncovered that would actually reopen Adele's case.

"The pictures," Roger whispered in his ear.

"The pictures!" Schwinn said with way too much excitement. "The pictures reveal a struggle and some clues that she wasn't alone." He was stretching the truth.

"Really?" Luke's mind was frantically trying to remember every detail of that night. "What kind of clues?"

"Look, Steven, I'm not prepared to have this discussion with you right now. My appointment is with Samantha. I didn't bring the file or pictures. Perhaps I can stop by tomorrow, and we can discuss this in detail. In the meantime, Samantha was supposed to download some stuff for me. I believe she put it on a flash drive." He was making it up as fast as he could think it through, just trying to keep them talking. "Could you please check her room to see if she left it for me?"

"Of course," Luke answered, looking to Madison to oblige so they could get rid of this guest.

"I doubt we'll find it. Samantha was never very good at cleaning her room," Madison protested.

"Past tense," Roger whispered in Schwinn's ear. "Bingo!"

"Well, I guess I'll try to reach her and see if I can reschedule. She hasn't picked up her phone all day. It just keeps going straight to voicemail. When's the last time you spoke with her?" he asked.

"Well, as I said, we've been out of state and just got home ourselves."

"You didn't answer my question," Schwinn pointed out.

"Why are you questioning me?" Luke countered. He could feel the sweat on his forehead and was doing his best to remain cool and collected.

158

FACE FRONT

Schwinn let out an easy laugh. "I'm sorry, Steven. Old detective habits die hard." He smiled and extended his hand once more before he headed for the door.

"I know," Luke replied. "And Samantha and I were so close, you just assumed I would know her every move." He shook Schwinn's hand and escorted him to the door.

"Did you catch that?" Schwinn whispered to Roger as he walked to his car.

"Yep, past tense," Roger replied with deep regret; he knew Schwinn was fond of Steven and wanted to believe in his innocence.

"And Rog, his hand was clammy," Schwinn said as he made his way down the long drive towards the street. "I don't want to believe it, Rog. I don't want to believe Steven was in on it."

"I know." Roger clicked off his phone as he got into Schwinn's car.

"I know this sounds crazy, Rog, but it was like Steven has turned into some sort of Stepford something or other." He sighed heavily. He couldn't explain it. "He was so formal, his speech, his actions; it was Steven, but like a plastic, stiff version of Steven." He sighed again, shaking his head for clarity. "It's the little things, like he referred to Adele as 'my late mother'. He always refers to her as

159

Adele. And Madison! He always calls her Madi." He knew he wasn't being clear. "Rog, I really hate this case," he admitted.

"I need to find a way to reopen Adele's death. We need help on this case. And we need to put Samantha is a safe house." Roger picked up his cell and dialed his chief.

CHAPTER 38

Grayson leaned over Samantha and kissed her forehead. This was rapidly becoming his trademark move for showing her affection without touching any of her tender bruises or stitches. She woke and turned to face him. "Did he call?" she asked.

Really? That's her first thought of the day? he thought. "No, beautiful," he replied, "I'm afraid not. Go back to sleep, it's ridiculously early."

"What time is it?"

"Five-thirty in the morning; much too early for you to be awake."

"You're going to work now?"

"Yes ma'am." He smiled at her. "But I promise you, Sammie, I will call you the minute I hear from him."

"Okay." She yawned. "Thank you."

"My dad is an early riser. He'll probably be up within the hour. My mom, well, not so much," he added with a slight laugh. "If you can't sleep, head to the kitchen and I'm sure dad will whip you up some breakfast; he's a great cook."

"Breakfast." She smiled and stretched. "Sounds lovely."

"It's too early; go back to sleep, you can have breakfast when you wake up again."

"Okay." She wiggled down into the covers and pulled them up around her chin. She felt so perfectly content. Within seconds she was asleep. She didn't even feel Grayson stroke her hair and kiss her forehead again before he left her room.

CHAPTER 39

"Good news, buddy." Roger said into his phone. "The Chief is reopening the case."

"Yes! I knew he would." Schwinn was excited and relieved to hear this latest development. He knew Adele's death was a murder, but he was hard pressed to prove it.

"We're on very limited resources, though," Roger continued. "He's going to communicate the details during the morning briefing. There's more; they found an explosive device wired into the engine of Madison's Mercedes. Driving off that cliff isn't what caused the car to blow. It seems the unit didn't function as intended. It was supposed to detonate seven minutes after the car was taken out of park. It should have exploded when Samantha was making her way into town, not on her return. The brakes not working was probably a side effect of a sloppy installation. Funny, though, because it's the very thing that saved her life."

"So you think Madison installed the unit?"

"That's a reach. She's such a princess; I just can't wrap my head around that."

"Steven then." He paused for a moment. "Steven attempted to kill his only child." He paused again. "For money, or love, or both."

"He had money," Roger pointed out. "He did it for greed."

"True," Schwinn agreed.

"There's more. We got a call from the LVPD. It seems they got a tip from a dumpsite, and they've recovered some items, including a computer, disposable cell phones, and shredded documents," he hesitated. "Poorly shredded documents," he corrected. "With the names Edward and Adele Montgomery on them. That's what led them to us. They overnight expressed the items to us. We pieced together a portion of the documents that connected both Adele and Steven with the name McCain. We've got people searching McCain's history."

"When do we move Samantha?"

"Today, she's safe for now. They don't even know she's alive. The Chief is going to fill Gray in on everything we know in about an hour, when he gets to the station" He looked at his watch. "Then he'll have him relocate her."

McCain, Schwinn thought. *Why does that name ring a bell?* He knew he'd heard it before. "Now that we know Steven is in on it, Rog, I'm going to go over my files again from a new perspective. Call me with anything new. I'll do the same."

"Copy," Roger replied and hung up.

164

CHAPTER 40

"Madison, you're driving me crazy," Luke protested.

"Dad, uh, Steven." she corrected herself. "Stay focused, this is important."

"I am focused. And I've been studying Steven for months. I've got it."

"You must know every minute detail," she pointed out again. "We can't leave too soon. It will look suspicious. So you have to live in Steven's world and function as he would. Once we've sold the house and moved away, you can be whatever version of Steven you want, but for now, you need to be the Steven Montgomery everybody knows. A deeply mourning version of him, who can no longer live in this house, this area, with all it's painful memories of Kate, Adele, and Samantha, but Steven Montgomery just the same."

"You're right, dear." He sat down on the loveseat across from her. "Don't you think I should call Samantha to see where she is?" He paused for a reply. When she didn't respond, he pressed on. "Wouldn't Steven call his daughter to find out why she wasn't home? Why she missed a scheduled appointment with his P.I.? Or wouldn't he at least return Grayson's call?"

"Yes," Madison agreed reluctantly. She did not want to make that call. She just wasn't up for dealing with it.

Luke pulled Steven's phone out of his robe pocket and hit Samantha's name on the caller speed dial. It went straight to voicemail as expected. "Sam, this is dad," he said into the phone just as he'd practiced with Madison. "It's seven o'clock. You must be sleeping. Call me when you wake up." He was just about to hang up when Madison mouthed *I love you.* "I love you," he said into the phone, and disconnected.

"Good job. You kept it brief; just enough for the police to see you as the concerned father who hasn't heard from your daughter, but not enough to give them anything to chew on."

"Shall we call Grayson now?"

"Might as well."

Luke walked over to the desk and picked up the piece of paper he'd written Grayson's phone number on. He plugged the numbers into his cell phone. "He may not want to deliver that kind of news over the phone," Luke said to Madison as he heard the phone ring.

"Mr. Montgomery." Grayson was so relieved Steven was returning his call. He knew this would make Samantha happy.

"Hello, Grayson."

"I only have a couple minutes. I have a mandatory briefing in less than five, but I need to talk with you. Are you alone by chance?"

This sparked Luke's interest. He glanced at Madison. "Yes, I'm alone," he lied.

"Have you seen the news?"

"No. I'm afraid I just got back from a business trip. I'm out of the loop. What's going on, Grayson?"

"The news will tell you there was a fatal car crash involving Madison Montgomery's vehicle and that it's believed Samantha was in the vehicle when it crashed. Don't worry!" he added quickly. "Sammie was in the vehicle, but she jumped out. She's pretty banged up, but she's alive and recovering." When Luke didn't say a word, Grayson continued. "Steven, I know this is hard, but please don't tell anyone she is alive. Not even Madison," he stressed. "We suspect someone tried to kill her, and we can't risk anyone, not even Madison, knowing she's alive." He paused for only a second. "Samantha insisted we tell you."

"Samantha is alive." Luke spaced each word out. His voice was weak and barely audible. He stared at Madison in shock.

"Yes. And please don't worry. She's safe. She's at my parents' house. I've got to run: the chief has started the briefing, and he's calling me. I will call you back after. Please don't tell anyone, not even Madison," he repeated. "I know this is hard to hear, but Steven, there is evidence Madison may be involved."

"Okay." Luke was in shock. "I will wait for your call." He hung up the phone and set it down on the table. He looked at Madison. "Samantha is alive."

"So I heard!" Madison's voice was pure venom.

"What are we going to do? She'll know within seconds I'm not Steven." Luke's voice was rising in pitch as he paced the floor in a panic. "This was a good plan, a thorough plan," Luke reasoned. "We worked on it for over a year!"

"We'll finish the job," Madison stated. "We have no choice."

"And how do you propose we do that without drawing more suspicion?"

"I don't know, but I think our first move is to get her back here where we can deal with her. We'll take the limo. That way I can be in the back without being seen. You'll go in the Ryan's home alone and get Samantha." She fired up her laptop as she was speaking.

"What are you doing?"

"I'm searching for the Ryan's address." She looked at Luke. "Call our driver, Seth. His number is in Steven's cell. I gave him a couple days off because I wanted you to get familiar before you had to meet the staff, but now we need him." She focused on her laptop again. "And get dressed!" she added in a huff.

Luke grabbed Steven's cell from the table and headed for his room.

Just twenty minutes later, Seth, always reliable, arrived at the front door with the limo ready to go. Madison handed Seth a piece of paper with the Ryan's address written on it. "We're in a hurry, Seth."

"Yes, Mrs. Montgomery." He rushed to open the door for her. Within minutes they were on the freeway heading for the Ryan's home.

"We should be there in ten, no more than fifteen minutes," Madison guessed. "It's not far."

"What if she instantly recognizes I'm not Steven?"

"You're identical. She's been in a very bad accident and is probably disoriented. Just hug her and guide her to the car. Try not to say too much."

Luke nodded his head in agreement. They rode the rest of the way in silence.

CHAPTER 41

"Rog, It's me," Schwinn said to Roger's voicemail. "Call me as soon as you get this message. I figured out where I've heard the name McCain. It's Madison's maiden name! She's Madison McCain! I can't figure out how Adele fits into all of this. Call me." He hung up the phone and turned back to his files.

"Hey, handsome." Miranda stood in the entryway of the dining room. "Didn't we have lunch and antique shopping plans this afternoon?" she asked.

"Miranda." Schwinn hated to disappoint his wife. He hated it more than antique shopping. "Hon, I'm..." He didn't know what to say. "Something is bugging me, and I can't place it. But I know I'm overlooking something," he tried to explain. "I feel Samantha Montgomery's life depends on it."

"Well, I guess I need to let you off the hook then." She could see he was genuinely struggling. "Can I help?" she offered.

"Yes! Sit right here and start reading through this stack of files. Hi-light anything you can find that has the name McCain on it." He handed her a yellow hi-lighter. The two sat side by side and worked in silence.

CHAPTER 42

When the limo pulled up in front of the Ryan's home, Gary was watering the front lawn. He knew instantly this must be Samantha's father. After all, not everybody traveled in that kind of luxury. "I'm Gary, Gray's dad." Gary introduced himself and shook Luke's hand. "Come on in, I'll ask Betty, my wife, to fetch Samantha." His voice was thick with a southern drawl.

Funny, Luke thought. *Steven never had a southern drawl. Guess good breeding didn't come with an accent,* he concluded. "It's nice to meet you, Gary," Luke replied and followed Gary inside the house.

"Betty Jean," Gary called out towards the kitchen. "Mr. Montgomery is here for Samantha."

"Please, call me Steven." Luke requested.

Samantha heard the exchange and rushed up the stairs, ignoring the mild pain it caused her. When she saw her father standing there, a wave of emotion hit her and tears began to run down her cheeks. She moved in close and hugged him tight. She felt him wrap his arms around her, but not nearly as tight as she wanted. Finally, after a long moment, she pulled back a little and looked up at him. "I know I look fragile, but really I'm not," she promised, hoping he'd stop being so cautious and hug her tighter.

"Are you ready to go home?" It was more of a prompt than a question.

"Yes. Do you think it's safe?"

"Of course it is, Samantha." His tone was condescending.

She pulled back a little further, staring at him. Something wasn't right, but she didn't know what. *Is it because of the accident?* She thought. *Has my appearance shaken him?* She tried to reason. *No, because Gray seems to act normal around me.* She leaned in close to him again and hugged him tight. "Daddy, I've been having those nightmares again. You know the ones, where I watch Mrs. Karp drown in our pool." She paused for a quick moment to see if he'd respond.

"It's only a dream."

"That was such a horrible accident," she pressed. "Do you think we could go to her grave and put some fresh flowers on it?" She pulled away again and looked up at him.

"Of course we can." He smiled down at her. "Now, let's go home and get you well."

FACE FRONT

"Let me get my things." She pulled completely away and headed downstairs to Gray's room. She tried to call Gray's cell, but it went to voicemail. She left a message, "Gray, my dad is here to pick me up, he wants to take me home, but something isn't right. I can't explain it. It's him, but he's not acting like himself. I know I'm not making sense, but something is wrong. Please call me right back." She hung up and slowly gathered her things.

When she got back upstairs, her father was having a casual conversation with Gary and Betty. Samantha stared at her father. *What's different?* She thought.

"You ready?" Luke asked.

"Ready." Samantha hugged Betty and Gary and thanked them for their hospitality. She was stalling: she didn't want to leave with him, but she had no idea what to do next. She needed Gray.

Gary and Betty escorted them out the front door and half-way up the drive. Betty was telling Samantha to please come back and visit.

"Oh, I forgot something." Samantha handed Luke her bag. "Dad, could you please have Seth put this in the trunk?" She turned her attention to Gary and Betty. "I have something I wanted to give you. You know, to thank you. I left it in Gray's room." She took a step towards the front door. "We'll just be a moment," she said to

175

Luke as she reached for Betty's hand and walked with her back inside the house.

"Well, it was nice to meet you," Luke said to Gary as he picked up Samantha's bag and headed for the limo. This was taking way too long, and his patience was starting to wear thin.

When Gary and Betty entered the house, Samantha closed and locked the door behind them. It startled both of them. "Samantha? Are you alright?" Betty asked.

"I know this sounds crazy, but something isn't right with my father. The nightmares I told him about, I made them up. I was testing him!" She was desperately trying to make them understand what she couldn't understand herself. "Mrs. Karp is our neighbor down the street. She walks her poodle and lets it poop on everybody's lawn. She is very much alive and annoys my dad daily." She looked at them, wild-eyed and desperate. "Don't you see? He agreed to go put flowers on her grave!"

"I'm calling Gray," Gary finally spoke up.

"I tried that. I got his voicemail."

"Then I'm calling the police." He grabbed the phone off the wall and tried Gray's number first.

"Dad!" Gray answered on the first ring. "Is Samantha alright?"

"Yes, son, she's here with your mother and me."

"Keep her there! We're on our way now!" Gray was practically yelling into the phone. "Detective Schwinn, he used to work with us, he went private, anyway, he discovered documents that Steven Montgomery was born Steven McCain and has an identical twin brother, Luke! Steven was adopted at birth, by Edward and Adele Montgomery, as a single."

"What?"

"Dad, listen carefully and do not repeat this to Sam. We suspect Steven is dead. I spoke to him this morning. Well, I thought it was him. Anyway, I told him Sam was alive and staying with you." He hesitated for just a second. "Dad, we think he may try to come to your home to kill Sammie."

"What?" Gary repeated.

"Oh, for Heaven's sake!" Betty was frantic trying to make sense of it, and Gary wasn't repeating any of his conversation with Grayson to her.

"Son." Gary stayed focused on Grayson. "He's here now. He's in his limo outside. Sammie was on her way out with him when she pretended to forget something and came back in the house. The three of us are holed up in here now."

"That's my girl!" Grayson exclaimed. "We're less than two minutes out. Just stay put. Go downstairs into my room out of sight in case it gets ugly. And Dad, don't tell Sam anything. This is not how I want her to hear it."

"Okay, son. We'll head downstairs now." As they hurried down the stairs, the front doorbell rang, it was an impatient, persistent sound. "Ignore that," Gary said, and just seconds later they could hear the sound of screeching tires in the front yard. "Get down on the floor," Gary instructed, pulling Leo, their dog, close to him as the three of them huddled together on the floor.

Samantha's body was shaking, and tears were running down her face. She could hear the police telling her father they had him surrounded. "I don't understand." She tried to control her trembling. "My father..." She couldn't finish her sentence.

With shaking hands, Betty was stroking Samantha's hair, trying to keep her calm. Her heart was breaking for Samantha. "It'll be over soon. Just stay calm." She tried to soothe Samantha.

Madison exited the limo and ran to Luke. She stood in front of him to protect him. "This is a terrible misunderstanding!" She yelled back to the police. "My husband only came here to pick up his daughter. She's been in a car accident."

"Luke and Madison McCain, you are under arrest for murder! Surrender immediately!" Boomed the voice over the loud speaker.

FACE FRONT

Madison felt the blood drain from her head. *How could they know?* she wondered. Her limo was surrounded by three police cars. The officer's were barricaded behind their cars with their guns drawn and aimed at her and her father. They had her limo driver, she observed. *How did they get Seth?* she wondered. "Daddy," she whispered. "It's over; we're going to jail." She felt like her head was in a fog. Everything seemed to be moving in slow motion. She reached into her pocketbook to silence her ringing cell phone. The bullet caught her directly above her left eye. She never even heard the gunshot. She was dead instantly.

When her body slumped to the ground, Luke fell to his knees beside her. "I surrender!" He cried. "I surrender!"

CHAPTER 43

Grayson sat in his father's oversized suede rocker recliner with Samantha wrapped in his arms, he gently rocked back and forth. He had no more words to offer her; he already shared everything he knew, and it left her broken. This he could not fix. He did the only thing he could; he held onto her tightly and waited for the storm of her latest loss to pass. When he finally felt her breathing become heavy and even, he knew she had cried herself to sleep. He reclined the chair back and closed his eyes; he felt exhausted. Knowing Samantha was in danger, and rushing to get to her, had his adrenaline running on high. The aftermath had left him completely drained. With Madison dead and Luke in jail, Samantha was finally safe. He could rest. Day turned to night, and night succumbed to the early morning dawn, and the two remained still, curled up in the recliner.

"Good morning," Grayson whispered as Samantha opened her eyes and blinked at the light pouring in from the living room's bay window. Her bruises were turning a very ugly mixture of yellow, brown, and purple; she looked more fragile than ever.

She leaned her head back on his shoulder. "What time is it?"

"Almost seven." He reached up and brushed away stray strands of hair that were covering her eyes. "Are you hungry?"

"No." She paused for a moment as she fought back a new day of tears. "I can't eat." Her voice cracked.

"Okay," he replied in a soothing tone.

"Is Luke still in jail?"

"Yes, he's not getting out anytime soon. Your father suspected something was wrong, and he hired a private investigator, a former police detective. He found evidence of birth records which showed your father and Luke were born identical twins. And he found adoption records for your father. We were able to match them to portions of the records Luke shredded, proving Luke was aware of these facts. Our technology department was able to recover Luke's hard drive, which is loaded with evidence against him: all of his research on the Montgomery family, his dealings with your father, and the like.

"My father's body?"

"The LVPD is recovering his ashes and sending them to us. We won't be able to determine cause of death, and so far Luke isn't talking, but we can at least give him a proper burial."

Samantha raised her head and looked Grayson in the eyes. "Thank you, Gray. Without you, I would be dead, and they would have gotten away with it. You trusted your instincts and you were right." She rested her head back on his shoulder. "What time do you go to work?"

"I don't," he was relieved to report. "Sam, I couldn't leave you like this, so I took a week of vacation time. You can stay here if you want. Or we can go away for a week, anywhere you want to go. Or I can take you home; I will stay with you as long as you need me to. It's your call."

She paused for so long, he thought she'd fallen back to sleep. "I think I'd like to stay here for another day. I know I need to go home, but I don't think I want to face that today."

"That's a good plan," he confirmed. He gently rocked her, while she cried silent tears.

CHAPTER 44

With her husband and all his case work moved back into his office, Miranda was dusting and enjoying the sheer beauty of her reclaimed dining room. She had spent a small fortune decorating this room, and she hadn't been able to see it, let alone enjoy it, for the past few months. Just thinking about the Montgomery case and that poor, sweet girl Samantha, made Miranda's spirit drop instantly. She decided to put down the dusting and go see if her husband was ready for a lunch break. When she walked into his office, she found him leaning back in his leather desk chair, with his feet on the desk. He was squinting to read the fine print of the newspaper he held in his hand. "Where's your reading glasses?" she asked.

"Can't find 'em."

"What? You just had them." She was searching her memory for when she saw him wear them last. She glanced around the room; everything was neat and tidy. She loved that about her husband: he was so organized. It was part of what made him so good at what he did for a living.

"They'll turn up."

"You're probably right. Are you hungry?"

"Always hungry," he pointed out.

"Do you want some left over lasagna?"

"There's some left?" He perked up. "I love your lasagna."

"Okay, meet me downstairs in about fifteen minutes." She turned to walk out of the room, then paused at the door. "We'll eat in the dining room." She smiled at him.

"Hey, Miranda, before you go." He gestured toward the newspaper. "Steven Montgomery's funeral is tomorrow morning. I think we should go."

She thought about it for a moment, then nodded her head in agreement. "I think you're right. What time?"

"Eleven. It's being held at Bethany. It's about a twelve minute drive."

"I'll be ready to go by ten-thirty," she promised.

"I love you," he called out as she headed down the stairs.

"I love you more," she called back as she descended the stairs. She headed to the kitchen to heat up their lunch and set the dining room table for two.

CHAPTER 45

It was an unseasonably warm day for the time of year. The thermostat read sixty-one degrees; there was a slight breeze in the air. If it had been under any other circumstances, the day would have been deemed perfect. But today Steven Montgomery's ashes would be laid to rest. Even the sunshine gave way to the dark cloud of the atmosphere surrounding this event. Samantha knew she needed to maintain her composure and take care of the business at hand; her father would expect her to be brave. But she wanted to stay holed up in that big, empty house she called home. She didn't want to face this part. She reached over and tucked her hand inside Grayson's. She was grateful she didn't have to face it alone. The first few rows were filled with close family friends, people Samantha grew up with, friends from school, Grayson's parents, his fellow police officers, Steven's business partners, and many significant members of the community; beyond that, the faces became a blur. The church was completely packed, and there were people standing on the front steps trying to make their way in. Steven had obviously been loved. "When our pastor asks me to come up and

187

say a few words, I may need you to walk with me," she whispered to Grayson. She wasn't sure her legs would carry her.

"Of course," Grayson replied. "Whatever you need."

Pastor Ron started the service by sharing with the crowd how generous Steven was to the church and the community. How deeply he would be missed, and how he was in Heaven now, with his wife, Kate, and his mother, Adele. He focused his attention on Samantha and promised her she would see him again someday. With that, he invited her up to say a few words. She found her strength. "I'm good," she reassured Grayson as she stood up and took her place at the podium. "I was blessed with an amazing father," she started her speech. "Well, actually amazing parents." She paused for a moment to clear the lump in her throat. "I know so many of you pity me right now for losing both my parents at such a young age, especially under the circumstances. I'm not going to lie to you: I've been battling with the thought of how unfair it feels. I think I was actually mad at God for allowing this to happen. But Pastor Ron is right; Second Corinthians promises us, 'to be absent from the body is to be present with the Lord.'" She paused and looked around the room. "I'm banking on that!" She felt her strength rising. "My father was never the same after my mother passed. There was a deep void in him; he missed her; and now, he's with her. They're together in Heaven, and someday I will see them again. My father's life was cut short, and it shouldn't have been, but I refuse to wallow in pity. Instead I choose to honor his memory and celebrate his life! I want to thank each and every one of you for coming today. I appreciate the love and support I've received. If there is anyone here who would like to share an uplifting experience you had with my father, please come join me." She lowered the microphone and stepped back from the podium.

One by one people approached the podium and told their favorite story portraying Steven Montgomery and his generosity, compassion, wonderfully funny personality, and much, much more. The crowd of mourners laughed, applauded, and at times, stood to honor him. Slowly, the dark cloud that hovered was forced to leave.

CHAPTER 46

"Okay, help me to fully understand this." Samantha lowered her head into her hands and rubbed her tired, blurry eyes. She was in the office of Caleb Carpenter, Attorney at Law. She was trying to make sense of what now belonged to her.

"Well, it's simple, really. Luke McCain, in an effort to make his suicide note believable, and with the intent to become Steven Montgomery, mortgaged his home, maxed out his credit cards, and took casino loans out against everything he had. He then took all that cash, roughly one point three million dollars, and purchased stocks using your father's name; he had, and used, your father's driver's license for identification purposes, which means they legally belonged to Steven Montgomery, and now, as his sole heir, they legally belong to you." Caleb Carpenter paused to make sure this was sinking in. "In addition, of course, to the monies you've already inherited from your late mother, grandmother, and father." He paused for another moment. "I'm sorry for your losses," he hastily added.

"One point three million," she repeated.

"Actually, Mr. McCain made some smart stock choices. If you cash out before close of business today, I believe you're looking at roughly one point seven million dollars."

Samantha leaned back in the chair. She gently rubbed her thumb over the fresh scar that crossed her cheek and mouth. "I don't know what I'm supposed to do next," she admitted.

"Samantha, I'm your father's attorney, well, your attorney. I'm good with the facts and legal consequences and outcomes, but I really can't advise you when it comes to monetary investments." He reached in his desk and pulled out a business card. "This is a financial advisor you should contact." He handed her the card. "I personally use him. He's good, real good; but he's expensive. You can afford him." He stood up and walked around to the front of his desk. He leaned on the edge of it. "Samantha, no amount of money is going to replace what Luke McCain stole from you. But you can't change the facts of the past; you can only move forward. This money is a small token of a payback. Go enjoy it. Use it to go back and finish school."

"Thank you, Mr. Carpenter." She stood up, shook his hand, and left his office, taking his advice with her.

CHAPTER 47

Luke McCain sat on a thin, dirty mattress in a small five foot by eight foot jail cell. It smelled of urine and sweat. He leaned back against the concrete wall and closed his eyes. "I can't spend the next thirty years living like this," he mumbled to himself.

"You may not have to." The voice with a heavy accent startled him; he opened his eyes to see a tall, bulked-up, dark-haired man wearing a guard uniform and aviator sunglasses.

"Who are you?"

"I'm the messenger. Mr. Greggori sent me; you've got three days."

"Three days!" Luke swallowed hard. "I can't come up with that kind of money in three days, especially not while I'm in here!" he protested.

The messenger leaned in close and wrapped his massive hand around Luke's throat. "You'll find a way."

"Samantha!" Luke cried. "Samantha Montgomery. She's got your money."

"We know the deal, McCain, don't even try it. We didn't do business with Samantha Montgomery, we did business with you." He released his grip and headed for the cell door. "Three days," he reiterated.

"You may as well kill me now." Luke hung his head. "I can't come up with the money in three days; I'm as good as dead."

"Oh, I'm not going to kill you," the messenger clarified.

"You're not?" Luke actually looked hopeful.

"Nope, the boss ordered me not to kill you; but I'm going to make you wish you were dead." The messenger turned and walked out the cell door, leaving a trembling Luke behind.

CHAPTER 48

It was a perfect day for a barbeque; late spring in South Carolina brought warm air, but no humidity. Kicked back on a whicker chaise lounge overlooking Schwinn's pool, Roger had no problem leaving the crime fighting to someone else; he was enjoying every minute of his day off. "Hat's off to the chef!" He nodded towards Schwinn. "This is delicious!" He took another bite of Cajun glazed chicken.

Miranda, sitting in a chaise beside him, agreed with a nod. She loved it when they barbequed; it meant she didn't have to cook. "Shall we tell him the real reason we invited him over for barbeque?" she asked her husband.

"Wait. This isn't a surprise blind date or anything, right?" Roger wiped his face. "Because sloppy barbeque is no way to meet somebody for the first time."

"No." Miranda was laughing at him. "Silly, Roger. I know better than that."

Schwinn took a break from the grill and sat at the foot of Miranda's chaise lounge. He pulled an envelope from the pocket of his button-down, camp shirt and handed it to Roger. "This is your half of the Montgomery case."

"What?" He took the envelope and stared at it. "You mean the fruit basket and thank you card you got four months ago wasn't payment in full?"

"Honestly, I thought she didn't know her father hired me. I wasn't about to spring it on her with all she'd been through. Miranda and I talked about it and decided to just cut our losses." He gestured toward the envelope. "Then we got a letter in the mail, explaining how she had to sort out some legal issues to gain access to her father's financials, and that she really appreciated our patience. There was a check for fifty thousand dollars."

"What?" Roger was shocked now.

"That's half." Schwinn pointed at the envelope Roger was holding.

Roger stood up and paced the ground around his chaise lounge, staring at the envelope. He finally stopped and looked at Schwinn and Miranda with the shock on his face turning to realization. "I think I'll take tomorrow off, too." He laughed raising his bottled beer. "Cheers." He gestured towards Schwinn and Miranda. "And, thank you."

"Thank you Rog." Schwinn countered. "I couldn't have done it without you." He touched his beer bottle to Roger's. "Seriously," he added. "I could not have proved this case and, in turn, saved Samantha's life without you. I think you should consider going private and teaming up with me."

"No." Roger smiled at his long-time friend. "If I went private with you, who would give you unpublished case facts?"

CHAPTER 49

Samantha and Grayson stood facing each other at the entry to the airport security line. "I'm going to miss you," Samantha finally broke the silence.

"Me too, Sammie. But I'm grateful you decided to go back to school."

"My dad would want me to finish."

"I know he would, and so do I." He lowered his forehead to meet hers. "We'll see each other in just a few months when you come home for Christmas." He was trying to sound upbeat.

"Yes. I'll be home for two weeks, Christmas through New Years." She didn't want to leave, but she knew she had to.

"What time's your flight?"

"Forty-five minutes."

"You'd better go then." He wrapped her in his arms and squeezed tight. He kissed her twice, then pulled away. "I love you, Sammie. Call me when you get there."

"I will." She kissed him once more. "I love you, too."

MILLIE MOORE

He watched her walk through the security line. He waited until she was completely out of sight before he turned and headed for the parking lot. He felt his cell phone vibrate in his pocket and smiled broadly when he recognized the New England phone number. "Hello, Mrs. Callahan, thank you for returning my call. I want to rent your bed and breakfast in Plymouth for the week of Thanksgiving. I'm going to surprise my girlfriend."

EPILOGUE

When Luke McCain discovered his brother, Steven Montgomery, he was jealous of Steven's life; he felt it was an unfair twist of fate. So instead of embracing his brother, and celebrating their reuniting, Luke chose to kill Steven. He wanted what Steven possessed; so he let his jealously and greed overrule his better judgment.

Luke McCain was a respectable business man with his own level of success; he was a building contractor. He lived in a nice home that he shared with his daughter, Madison McCain, but the fruit of his jealousy and greed produced discontentment in his life. In an effort to take what belonged to his brother, he lost what belonged to him.

Luke McCain was sentenced to life without parole. He now lives in a small jail cell without even the basic luxuries of life. His jealousy and greed have cost him his most precious possessions, his daughter, Madison, and his freedom. He would prefer to be dead.

AFTERWORD

Genesis 4: 6-15 (The Amplified Bible)

6 And the Lord said to Cain, Why are you angry? And why do you look sad and depressed and dejected?

7 If you do well, will you not be accepted? And if you do not do well, sin crouches at your door; its desire is for you, but you must master it.

8 And Cain said to his brother. Let us go out to the field. And when they were in the field, Cain rose up against Abel his brother and killed him.

9 And the Lord said to Cain, Where is Abel your brother? And he said, I do not know. Am I my brother's keeper?

10 And [the Lord] said. What have you done? The voice of your brother's blood is crying to Me from the ground.

11 And now you are cursed by reason of the earth, which has opened its mouth to receive your brother's [shed] blood from your hand.

12 When you till the ground, it shall no longer yield to you it's strength; you shall be a fugitive and a vagabond on the earth [in perpetual exile, a degraded outcast].

13 Then Cain said to the Lord. My punishment is greater than I can bear.

14 Behold, You have driven me out this day from the face of the land, and from Your face I will be hidden; and I will be a fugitive and a vagabond and a wanderer on the earth, and whoever finds me will kill me.

15 And the Lord said to him. Therefore, if anyone kills Cain, vengeance shall be taken on him sevenfold. And the Lord set a mark or sign upon Cain, lest anyone finding him should kill him.

CPSIA information can be obtained at www.ICGtesting.com
Printed in the USA
LVOW13s2309030414

380197LV00006B/6/P